MAXIMUS

GUARDIAN SECURITY SHADOW WORLD
BOOK FIFTEEN

KRIS MICHAELS

Copyright © 2024 by Kris Michaels

All rights reserved.

No part of this book may be reproduced in any form or by any electronic or mechanical means, including information storage and retrieval systems, without written permission from the author, except for the use of brief quotations in a book review.

❦ Created with Vellum

CHAPTER 1

*D*emos stood up, cheering for his grandson. The kid would be a major league pitcher one day if his dad, Demos' son Allen, didn't push him too hard. He'd temper his son's enthusiasm. Hard to do when Allen was one of the best outfielders New York had ever produced.

When his phone vibrated in his pocket, he answered it without looking. "That's what I'm talking about!" he cheered as his grandson threw strike out number three. "Hello?"

Demos' attention snapped from the game to the gravelly voice on the phone. "Hold on, let me get some distance from the stands." He looked at his wife. She narrowed her eyes and then nodded. She knew who was on the phone. Thank God she was the most patient person on the planet. Working for Guardian, he'd put her through the wringer, but she'd never complained. Not once in all the years he'd worked for Gabriel had she mentioned the birthdays or holidays he'd missed when he was recruiting for the organization.

He walked a good distance away from the stands and leaned against a big cottonwood tree. "What's up?" There was no need for pleasantries. Although he respected Jason as much as he respected Gabriel, they weren't close in the way he was close with the man who'd changed his world.

"Do you have contact with Maximus?" Jason King asked.

"I always do. Why? Isn't he answering you?" Demos glanced at the field when he heard an explosion of cheering. Damn, sounded like he missed one hell of a hit.

"No." Jason sighed. "I'm assuming he's working."

"He does get consumed in whatever career he's chosen at the moment. Do you have a mission for him?"

"Abrasha Molchalin."

"How?"

"That's for Maximus to tell us. I'm releasing him to do this however he deems necessary." Jason was silent for a moment. "We need him to assess the man, find his weakness, and exploit it to get to him. He's a violet code if necessary."

Demos looked up at the white clouds floating over the baseball park. It was too fucking nice out to think about the casualties a violet code authorized. "Damn. Violet. Okay, I'll get ahold of him."

"How's the grandson's pitching?" Jason asked.

"Better and better. He's going to go places." Demos didn't even try to hide the pride in his voice. His family was everything to him.

"I'm happy for all of you. Thanks for taking the time to reach out to Maximus for us."

"No problem. He'll call you by nightfall."

"That works. Archangel clear." Demos glanced down at the phone. Damn, it was still strange to hear anyone but Gabriel use that term. But then again, he was old school. His assassins were the old guard. Lycos was recruiting the new ones, and he was doing a damn good job. He had a different way of looking for recruits. Technology was impressive, but Lycos still did the one-on-one. A computer couldn't replace gut feelings or that sense that crawled up your spine when you knew someone wasn't the fit. He'd walked out of hundreds of meetings without offering someone a chance with Guardian. A person just … knew … At least he and Lycos did, and that was all that mattered.

***

MAXIMUS STARED at the screen and then smiled. "Got you, motherfucker." He hit a key on his keyboard and then watched as his code flew across the screen. He studied the Chinese language on the screen and watched as the hacker in China scrambled to save his systems. It was a futile effort. "And that's what you get for trying to crack into one of my systems, sir."

"Boy, don't you answer your phones?" Demos' voice behind him was expected. He knew the second his dad was on his property.

"Been kind of busy keeping this asshole out of the White House's national security system." Max continued to watch as the code he'd written destroyed the systems, twelve systems to be exact, that had mounted an attack. It was a common occurrence, but that one had gone further than any others. He'd decided it was time to teach the assholes a lesson.

"Doesn't the White House have operators who

could do that?" Demos came in and sat down beside him.

Max frowned. They did. But … "I was bored. Sue me."

"You could have come to the game, and you missed a call from Archangel."

"No, I didn't. I saw it. Just figured my priority was taking care of our nuclear arsenal. Jewell and Con don't have any issues at the moment. And you know I don't like the way Allen pushes Brent. It makes me itchy." Itchy and him didn't agree. Itchy was a very bad thing. He'd learned to police that feeling.

"I had a talk about that with Allen before I came here. Don't think he realized what he was doing. We'll see if bringing it to his attention helps. Hope it does."

"If not, let Mom take it on."

Demos laughed. "Don't tempt me."

Max leaned back and turned toward his dad. "What did Archangel want?" He looked at his monitor of Guardian's systems. He didn't see any issues.

The smile slipped off his father's face instantly. "They don't want Max; they want Maximus. Your target is Abrasha Molchalin."

Max cocked his head. Well, it was about time, and since he was bored to death, he could use the diversion. "Interesting. I make all the calls and assign any secondary duties. No one questions it. I'm not checking with anyone."

Demos nodded. "Which is why this target is yours. The Council has violet-coded the bastard. They want you to find his weakness, exploit it, and take him down. You have Val, Smithson, Flack, or any of the class to assist you."

"To assist me." Max snickered at the thought. "In doing what?"

"In taking this man down. He travels with an army. You know that. The hit is yours, but you'll need help."

Max laughed. "I think I may be insulted."

Demos snorted. "Deal with it. He's slipped through Guardian's hands too many times. This time, you'll take him out, and the others will clear the path to him. You get there, read the situation, and then call in the reinforcements. No lone wolf here. You copy?"

"I copy. I don't like it, but I understand the rationale." Maximus turned back to his keyboard and took one last glance at the situation he'd shut down in China. Those operators would probably cease to exist. Most of the people who failed epically in governmental computer attacks disappeared. Was there a twinge of regret? Not even a glimmer.

"Give me a minute, Pops. Let me do some digging." He typed for a few moments and read the output of his system. He had the most advanced system in the world, which was child's play to maintain and update. His entire basement was nothing but one secure system, with redundancy and generator power, shielded by a mesh system he invented. Only Saint had a similar system—much smaller but similar.

"Take your time. I like watching you make the computer do somersaults and backflips."

Max chuckled. "Then hold on. We're going to stick the landing."

His dad had found him when he was trying to survive. His aunt had been murdered in a random act of violence. No one had told him. He had to find out by using the computer his aunt had bought for him and searching the NYPD's database when she didn't come home. He'd grieved her loss for a week and then decided he'd take care of himself because no one had showed up to take him away. Only, at twelve, he'd failed to anticipate two variables. Those variables had led Demos to him, alone in the apartment his aunt rented. With no options for employment at his age, he'd obtained funds by breaking into the banking system and hitting the biggest account he could find. Gabriel Alexander had owned that account. Someone with that much money wouldn't miss a couple thousand dollars—or so he'd thought. He'd used the money to pay rent for the next six months via direct deposit. Mistake number one. The second mistake had been depositing money in his aunt's account because she'd kept a spare debit card in her top dresser drawer. Demos had arrived at his door twenty-four hours later. The man had sat him down and talked to him like an adult, which he'd respected. With his intellect, most people either assumed he was weird or developmentally challenged.

He wasn't. Usually, he was bored with a conversation within seconds, and he tuned out whoever was in front of him to work on interesting problems in his mind. After he'd admitted to Demos what he'd done, the man had offered to take care of him. To provide him with the education and resources to develop his gifts. Since that day, he'd been raised with Demos' family. He had younger brothers and sisters who loved him and accepted him. Demos had ensured he'd had challenges, but he'd never pushed.

He'd guided his development, and his sense of right and wrong, good and evil, had been shaped through his interactions with Demos and Guardian. The agency had fully employed him as their security system engineer when he was fifteen. He'd developed all their systems and taught Jewell by using an untraceable online persona when she'd first came aboard, guiding her and the agency when requested.

Demos waited quietly as he worked. The man never rushed him. He never pushed him but was there to encourage him and to listen, even though he didn't understand a word Max said. Venting was what Demos called it, and more times than not, venting led him to a solution for his problem.

Max finished his assessment, turned, and looked at the only father he'd ever known. "His weakness is his love of art."

Demos frowned. "Explain that for me, please."

Maximus chuckled. "From what I can find, he employs a curator, which means he loves art and presumably has an extensive collection. The curator has held several private showings, which, by following logic, would mean the curator is showing portions of his collection. The way to Molchalin is through art."

"How did Guardian not know this?"

"They probably haven't been able to tap into the Russian government's State central system or haven't needed to do so. Once there, I was able to filter for any mention of Molchalin. Of course, there weren't any. So, I started to look for influxes of money, non-State related. The Russian State museum had several large and recent donations from a curator, Elena Ivanova, to continue the restoration of old easel paintings. There were other donations from private citizens I also followed. However, Ivanova was the most interesting. She has a masters degree in art history from Saint Petersburg State University and is currently paid by a series of shell companies. All the other donations indicated are from banking institutions outside of Russia, which is normal for the rich of Russia. They don't keep their money in Russia."

"So, the curator is employed by Molchalin?" Demos leaned forward.

"Yes. Based on the information Jewell and Con have found and tagged in Guardian's system, I could piece the shell companies together and trace it back to Molchalin." Maximus looked back at the screen. "From the records I've uncovered, she's been employed by his system of shell companies for the last four years."

Demos whistled. "And she hasn't been killed. That's pretty amazing."

He nodded in agreement. Most who worked with Molchalin didn't last long. He watched with interest as the events involving Molchalin unfolded. Jewell and Con were good at what they did, but there was one he'd had his eye on—a genius with computers. Not exactly where Max was intuitively, but someone he thought was being underused and underappreciated. He'd bring that up when the mission was over.

"Do you have anything else?"

He blinked back to the conversation. He'd heard everything—he always did. However, his brain tended to work faster than most conversations. "The way in is through his art collection. He has a vested interest in the art and either respects the curator's abilities, or she's just as evil as he is. Either way, she's the weak link."

Demos nodded. "How will you exploit her to get in?"

Max shrugged. "I'll become an art expert and make myself a cover persona." It would be something he hadn't studied before, and it should be entertaining to mess around with a persona again.

Demos smiled. "How long will that take you?"

Max narrowed his eyes and thought about the

extent of knowledge needed. He'd need to know enough to have a discourse about any painting. The eras, the artists, the current market, and the nuances of an exhibit, plus he'd need to know all the major players in the art world. "I can be ready in a month. Less if needed, but I'd be comfortable with a month."

Demos chuckled. "Have I ever told you your brain amazes me?"

"Continuously." Maximus chuckled.

"Well, it's true, but remember, while your brain is special, *you* are more important than anything your brain can do. You're the person we love, and you're the person who's essential to our family." As Demos stood up, he followed suit. He was taller than his father and had more muscle, but he didn't doubt for a second Demos could put him on his ass if he weren't careful. They worked out and sparred together, and Demos was a force to be reckoned with. His dad grabbed him and gave him a rib-crushing hug. "Mom wants you to come to dinner tonight. We're celebrating Brent winning his game. A no-hitter."

"I'll be there. I probably need to call Archangel and fill him in on what I've found and what I plan to do."

"Yep. That was the request." His dad clasped him

on the shoulder. He leveled a stare in his direction. "Do not under any circumstance put yourself in a position that would get me in trouble with your mom. If you go over to Russia and get yourself killed, you know what'll happen to me."

"Yeah, you'd be in the afterlife with me in two seconds."

"That is the honest-to-God truth. I'm not afraid of many people, but your mom is one person we never cross."

"Don't I know it? I'll be over for dinner." Since he lived three houses down the block, getting there in time wouldn't be a hardship.

"If you don't show up, I'll send Martha over."

"Dad, for God's sake, don't even threaten that. Get out of here. I'll be over." He laughed and picked up his phone. His little sister was a pest of the largest order and thought he needed a girlfriend. The epic failures of Martha trying to fix him up were now well-told stories at family get-togethers. Mom had banned her from trying again.

CHAPTER 2

*E*lena Ivanova filled her lungs with fresh air as she walked along the seaside promenade in Sochi, Russia. At sunset, the Caucasus Mountains were a stunning backdrop. The gold, orange, and red hues peeked around the mountain tops, saturating the vistas with colors artists had tried to capture since time began. She tucked her hands into her jacket's pockets. Although spring was well underway, the air was cool, especially after spending the day in a climate-controlled vault.

Stopping at her favorite café, she took her normal table. The waitress would bring her a pot of tea, and she'd work on her emails while waiting for dinner. She could afford to eat out, and her employer ensured it. The day had been long but rewarding. That morning, she'd sent her boss a video of the newly acquired art, assuming he was out of town. But he wasn't, and he showed up at the vault an hour later. She showed him every painting, and they went over each one. While she logged the work, Abrasha would quiz her about the origins, the artists, the value, and whether or not each piece was show-worthy. Her vast knowledge of the art she bought for him and her learned knowledge of his preferences had resulted in a collection that was second to very few—except for the handful of paintings she stored deep inside the vault. Those paintings were problematic, but Abrasha didn't want to hear her concerns.

She took off her coat and thanked Marissa, the café owner, for her tea. While she let the leaves steep, she stared out the window at the promenade. Even as dusk grew into darkness, people walked down the palm tree-lined venue. She smiled at the thought of palm trees in Russia. Sochi was subtropical, and the average temperature along that area of the Black Sea was temperate enough to support the beautiful aesthetic.

She noticed a man sitting at a table just past her as she poured her tea. He was larger than the average male and wore round, wire-rimmed glasses. He ordered tea and his meal. Elena lifted an eyebrow at the American accent. Curious, but not completely unheard of. Some of the more affluent Americans had discovered the beauty of the Russian Rivera, as Sochi was called. Her eyes were drawn to the man. His dark brown hair was combed neatly, and the cloth of his suit jacket stretched over the breadth of his shoulders. The fabric was expensive, and the crisp linen of his shirt collar and cuffs was brilliant white. The aesthetic contrasted against his red tie was eye-catching, to say the least. He turned a bit, and she noticed the angle of a strong jaw. However, he didn't look around. Instead, he was intensely focused on whatever he was reading.

Elena opened her small laptop to start going through her emails. They'd stacked up as she'd worked on creating the interpretive language for the descriptions of the paintings they'd received. Her employer wanted the descriptions within seventy-two hours of receipt of the art. Of course, she could use the work of others, but that wasn't what she was being paid for. Abrasha wanted her words and her product. She wasn't fool enough to take any short-cuts. Her employer had specific requirements, which she provided, and in return, she was paid very well. That was something she kept in the forefront of her mind. Dealing with Abrasha was always a chess game.

The man put down the document he was reading, and Elena's curiosity was piqued as she glanced at the papers, which she recognized immediately. It was a Sotheby's brochure for what looked like a private sale. She'd seen the documents many times and had sold and purchased privately through the company. The painting depicted on the open page was fabulous and highly sought after by her employer. She hadn't been able to coordinate even the opening stages of negotiation for the *Salvator Mundi*. Although the pedigree of the painting was highly contested, and the debate still continued to this day, she didn't care if da Vinci painted it or one of his students had; the painting was on the top of Abrasha's list.

She picked up her teacup and walked to his table. Being a retiring wallflower was never her strong suit, and when an opportunity presented itself, she wouldn't walk past it. "I see you are an art lover." She spoke in English, which she'd learned from her mother and perfected while living and attending school in England before enrolling in St. Petersburg State University. Having a mother who was a British citizen and a father who was a Russian citizen gave her the best of both worlds.

When he frowned and looked confused, she nodded to the picture depicting the *Salvator Mundi*. His eyes cut to the folder and then back to her. My God, the thrill of excitement rushed over her like a wave crashing the shore, nearly knocking her to her knees. The man turned the document over. "Perhaps."

Elena nodded to the chair next to him. "May I?" She really did need to sit down. The man was handsome from a distance. Up close, he was ... magnetic —or perhaps incendiary was a better word.

He hesitated but nodded, and she sat down as gracefully as she could, hoping her tea wouldn't slosh over the lip of her cup as she made the move. Drawing a reinforcing breath, she continued, "The *Salvator Mundi* was last sold for four-hundred-fifty million dollars."

"I am aware." The man poured his tea that had been steeping.

"Perhaps I should introduce myself. I'm Elena Ivanova. I'm a curator for a private collector here in Russia." She extended her hand.

The man took her hand in his. "Max Stryker." The warmth of his hand and the strength of his handshake were a strong indication of his almost over-the-top masculinity. The man was breathtaking up close, but she was focused on the painting.

"Are you a curator or a collector?" She took a sip of her tea, trying to calm her heartbeat. The painting was causing the excitement, not the man. At least, that was what she told herself.

Max cocked his head and stared at her for a moment. "Why would you need to know?"

She smiled. He was making her work for it. She loved a challenge, and that pulled her away from the insane initial attraction she felt to the man. Which was good. She couldn't and wouldn't fall for any romantic entanglement. She had goals for her life, and a man was not on that or any other agenda. As she leaned forward, her hair slipped over her shoulder, and she noticed Max's eyes followed the fall of brown hair, which was unusual because she wasn't what anyone would call a beauty. She was far too curvy to be considered beautiful in the day and age of stick-thin fashion. Her lips were too full, and having brown hair and hazel eyes was about as boring as possible. She tossed that thought away as she leaned forward to answer his question. "If you were a curator, I'd ask to be included in any consideration for the sale of that work of art. If you were a collector, I'd ask you to meet my employer, who would love to discuss the procurement of that painting."

His eyes traveled to her cleavage, then up to meet her gaze. "I'm not a curator, but I work in acquisitions for a rather large conglomerate of collectors with Middle Eastern origins."

Her insides crawled at that look. No, never again. That was why she had very strong boundaries. Her goal was the painting, not a night of hot sex. His answer explained why the *Salvator Mundi* would be in the material the man was holding. It was rumored a Middle Eastern prince had purchased the painting. But she still needed an opening. She tried another tactic. "The provenance of the painting has always been contested." She leaned back in her chair and took a sip of her tea.

A twitch of a smile flitted at the corner of his mouth. "A four-hundred-year gap between creation and market does raise eyebrows for some. Of course, the ownership is not contested now, and the value is not questioned," Max said and lifted an eyebrow.

The gesture made the man even more handsome if that were possible. She smiled and then laughed. It was fun to talk to someone who spoke her language. "Which, in our terms, means the painting is expected to sell for more than it was purchased for." She tipped her head to him and added, "I happen to know a certain entity who would be interested in purchasing that particular painting."

Max chuckled. It seemed he also appreciated the conversation, but his next words dashed any hope she might have had. "I'm afraid you'll have to join a very long line of people who want but cannot have."

"Alas, I believe my collector does have the money to play in this arena, but I understand. A girl can dream, can't she?" Elena tried to play off the disappointment. If she could score even an appointment for Abrasha to discuss the purchase of the painting, she would be rewarded handsomely, and then she'd leave and find a position at a reputable gallery. Being the curator at a museum had always been her plan. Her contract with Abrasha was for five years, and she wouldn't renew it. Her employer was a very powerful and very controversial Russian billionaire. She heard the rumors, the whispers at the showings, the subtle moves away from him, and she saw the fear in people's eyes when he was present. Her father had warned her not to take the position and had told her horrible stories related to the man, but she'd needed the job and experience.

Abrasha stated his expectations, and as long as

she met them, there were no problems. She'd witnessed his ugly side at a showing when someone had said something he didn't like. After that explosion, the chill in the air would have frozen the Siberian tundra ten times over. She didn't host a showing for over a year after that event. She didn't know what was said, but she did know the offender, and he was found dead shortly afterward. A heart attack was the official cause; it wasn't what was said in her circles, though. Many had warned her to walk carefully around her boss.

Taking a sip of his tea, Max leaned back in his chair. "Dreaming gains little traction in our work, I'm afraid. All our interested parties have been vetted. Would your employer be able to pass through those gates? We don't let people who can't afford the price of entry into the discussion. A necessary business decision, as I'm sure you're aware."

Elena blinked, leaned forward, and whispered, "Truly, are you suggesting there's a chance my employer could be included in that discussion?"

Max looked around the small café. "I don't know you. You don't know me. I suggest we both do our due diligence before assuming any proposed invitation."

Elena nodded. "I believe you're correct." She

reached into her pocket and extracted a thick, gold-painted, bevel-edged business card. "My contact information. I can provide my employer's details."

Max reached inside his coat pocket and retrieved his card. It was black, made of metal, and had only a number etched in the medium. "You can follow the instructions at this number to leave documentation proving your client is in the league he needs to be. I'll get back to you when I'm able."

His dinner was placed in front of him. She smiled and placed the card in her pocket. "I'll let you eat in peace. It was fortuitous to meet you here tonight."

Max smiled politely and admitted, "Strange, I thought it was a bit *too* fortuitous."

Elena's smile slipped from her face. *Wait. What?* "You don't think I was following you, do you?" She pointed to her table, where her dinner was getting cold. "I was sitting there when you came in, and you can ask anyone here; I come in most nights and have for the last four years."

Max seemed to consider her words before nodding. "My apologies if I have offended you, but you must admit, the likelihood of both of us in one place at one time is ... illogical."

"I would prefer to think of it as fate." Elena stood.

"I hope to hear from you if I pass your background checks."

"And I hope you also do your due diligence, Ms. Ivanova." He put his papers in the slimline briefcase he had with him before tucking it under the table and beginning his meal. She blinked at the action and turned back to her table. *As if she would try to steal the document?* Floored by the actions, she dropped back into her seat, activated her computer screen, and stared at her email. *What an insult.* She was well-known in the area. She had contacts and could give the man referrals, but if he wanted to do his checks, so be it. Her integrity was beyond reproach in the art world.

She choked down a meal she couldn't taste and left before Mr. Stryker. She wasn't sure if she was more excited about the chance or offended by the sexy man's actions. She took several long, calming breaths. He didn't know her and only had her word that her client could enter the exalted world where he worked. Would she have reacted the same way? Perhaps. No, definitely, she would have been suspicious. As she walked home, excitement about the possibility of an opportunity grew, but she needed to tamp it down. She wouldn't breathe a word of her meeting. She didn't want to jinx it, but the possibility of being considered into the conversation of purchasing the *Salvator Mundi* was a lifetime accomplishment.

The walk to her oceanside apartment took only a few minutes. She opened the door and turned on the lights before hanging up her coat and dropping onto her couch. She connected to the true internet, not the Russian State internet, which Abrasha had provided for her at her residence and work. She needed to research Mr. Max Stryker.

For the next two hours, she consumed every article that mentioned the man. Most articles mentioned prestigious acquisitions in the art world, including Max's work. There were old pictures where he was usually in the background. She smiled as she noticed that any reference to him was always with the highest regard. Closing the computer, she stared out her window. *If she could only get her foot in the door.* Her employer's art portfolio was extensive, and he was a billionaire. By all accounts, Abrasha Molchalin could sit at any table with the richest of men. She would provide the documents and hope for the best.

Rising to get ready for bed, she turned off the light, then walked to the window overlooking the Black Sea. The reflection of the moon danced off the water. She glanced at the canvas to her left. She'd captured the scene in oil and watercolors several times. She was talented but not nearly enough to be considered a rising artist. Her paintings would never be hung in galleries, but she found peace and beauty in creating a scene that pulled at a person's imagination.

She ran her finger over the canvas-wrapped frame and smiled. Beauty was in the eye of the beholder. People with money also dictated what was beautiful and what wasn't. In her opinion, the *Salvator Mundi* was not up to da Vinci's standard of art. She didn't agree with those who said he painted it. The features were not sharp or defined in true da Vinci fashion, nor was the torso twisted, which was his norm. There was also a problem with the glass orb. Distortion wasn't present, and da Vinci would have used the glass to reflect such a thing. As a master, da Vinci wouldn't have missed that nuance. No, she believed that perhaps the master's student had painted the most expensive painting in the world, but her opinion didn't matter. Abrasha's opinion and desires did, and she'd explained her concerns about that specific painting to him ad nauseum. She'd do it again if they were presented the chance to bid on the painting.

Her mind wandered back to the man who'd awakened her very dormant libido, even if it was momentarily. He was possibly the most interesting person she'd met in years. The sensations when he looked at her were so immediate and overwhelming. Narrowing her eyes, she glanced back out at the sea. It was vast, beautiful, enticing, and exciting, like Max. Yet she wouldn't swim in the sea because there were unseen dangers to those who weren't strong swimmers. She wasn't. Perhaps it would be wise to remember that fact. Her talents didn't involve swimming or relationships. She'd stick to what she knew.

CHAPTER 3

aximus took off his jacket and made his way into his hotel room. He opened his suitcase, unfastened the false bottom, and extracted his equipment. Sweeping the room was his priority. Although the chances of someone installing monitoring equipment in the room while he was gone were slim, he wasn't taking any risks. He'd disabled the listening devices by turning on a high-frequency jamming cube resembling an electrical adapter. He'd developed the technology last year, which was now standard issue for all Guardian Shadows working in Russia and throughout the world.

Loosening his tie, he ensured the room was clean before returning to his phone and calling up an app he'd developed. He tapped on it and watched as Elena Ivanova worked on her computer. The woman was quite a revelation. Her English rather than Russian accent wasn't anticipated, although he knew her mother was British, and she'd attended school in England before returning to Russia. Another revelation proved to be his immediate and unwavering interest in the woman. Unwavering being the keyword. Why and how did that happen? Only a handful of people held his attention beyond the first interaction. People were slow, boring, and uninteresting. Yet she wasn't, which was something he needed to decode. Not knowing why he had an interest made him itchy. He didn't like that sensation.

His cameras, which he'd installed that morning, operated perfectly. The woman's security was next to nonexistent. Wearing a pair of gray overalls, he'd carried a toolbox and walked into her building. No one had questioned him, and the lock on her door had taken seconds to defeat. The apartment was small but neatly appointed. He'd used his time to install three cameras and get to know his mark. She was tidy. Dishes had been done and put away. Her bathroom had been clean, and there were minimal beauty products that she didn't need. She was a beautiful woman.

He'd gone through her closets, dresser, and every cupboard in her apartment. Volumes of art books had lined the shelving units in her living room. The desk area had been neat. There'd been papers on leasing a hall, and he'd noted the date. If she were planning a showing, it would fit his plan nicely. Assuming he could get an invitation, which he believed he could, his access to Molchalin would be almost guaranteed. With the asshole being violet coded, all the people at the show were expendable. Using the resources he had available, he could trap his prey while the others handled Molchalin's army of security. Escape from that public execution could be problematic, however, without a specific plan for everyone, especially because he would take his time and leave the message Guardian wanted. No one was untouchable. No one, including the Shadows. That was why he still worked so damn hard for Guardian. He made sure Shadows were not traceable. Well, unless they gave out their address. He'd had words with Malice about that slip. He'd also used the information Honor had given Jewell to reinforce the programs that would swoop in if Jewell's defenses failed. He'd taken on the overall system because Gabriel had asked him to do so after the Siege. He'd also bring on someone to train under him so the safety net never faltered.

He'd continued his work in Elena's apartment. There had been nothing unanticipated until he'd tested her internet. Most people accessed the State's internet via wireless hookup, so the port at her desk was a novelty. He'd opened his toolbox and pulled out the equipment he needed. Plugging in a stand-alone computer, he'd sent out a signal. What he'd received in return was interesting. Her access to free-world internet aside, what had caught his attention was that her access was more than likely being monitored. It was a private network, so decrypting traffic at a proxy was a no-brainer. No doubt, that was a common occurrence when one worked for Abrasha Molchalin. That being said, as soon as he made contact, Abrasha could know about it, particularly if she did any research on him, which he hoped she would. He'd quickly installed his monitoring system so he could see what she did on the computer, closed the wall plate, and made sure everything was returned to normal. Then he'd pulled his phone out, accessed his app, and looked at himself in the woman's apartment. Walking into the kitchen and finally into the bedroom, he'd ensured he had adequate coverage before exiting the apartment.

Now, sitting in his hotel room, he studied the woman. He anticipated at least three or four near misses or brush-bys before they would make contact, so her approach was intriguing. She was more attentive than he'd anticipated, which made the contact more entertaining. He changed the app and accessed his secure texts.

> CONTACT MADE.

HE SENT the message and closed the app. He didn't care if anyone acknowledged it, nor was he obliged to check in with a handler. He controlled all Guardian's systems; checking in with anyone coming to assist was almost useless. He could access any information he needed, and he knew his help was en route and would be in Sochi by the night's end tomorrow. With the first contact made, he would study more and meet with the Shadows who arrived. Separately or a rendezvous of all hands, he didn't care.

But his pops got antsy if he didn't check in

through the system now and again. Both his dad and Guardian knew what they released when they released him. His analytical brain didn't register the empathy that most people showed when dealing with humans. Unless he had a connection with a person, there was little … there was no concern about their pain or predicaments, which allowed him to send statements without a moral dilemma that ninety-nine-point-nine percent of the population would be forced to endure.

When his phone rang, he closed his eyes before lifting it to his ear and answering. "Yes?"

"You didn't call to let us know you'd arrived." His father's voice on the other end of the line made him smile.

"I don't check in. You know that."

Demos' voice lowered. "You do when your mom thinks you're traveling for business, and that's what you told her." His voice lifted to normal tenor. "So she wants to know you're safely in London."

"Ask her to forgive me. I started work as soon as I got in." Which wasn't a lie. "I'll call when I'm heading home, but I probably won't have time to check in."

He could hear his mom taking the phone away from his father. "I was worried."

"Not a problem, Mom. But I could be over here

for months. I'm not sure how long the company will need my assistance. I'll call when I can, but I'll be busy for the next few weeks. Day and night."

"Well, that stinks. Won't you get to see any of the sights?"

"Not at first. Maybe later. I'll be okay, Mom."

"You work too hard."

"Work isn't hard." He laughed.

"Well, for you, maybe not, but that doesn't mean you need to do it all the time. You should be out meeting people your own age."

"I promise I'll get a bit of play in, too." He knew what his mom was hinting at, but any future concepts didn't have a significant other in them as far as he was concerned. Even so, his mind flitted to the beautiful brunette with the proper English accent. She was his version of damn near perfect. If she had a security clearance, she'd be perfect. But even if he wanted a relationship, one could never happen for many reasons. Most importantly, he had no idea how to function in a relationship other than what he'd seen of his mother and father. He watched and learned, but the connection they had with each other, and with him and their other children, was special. He wasn't sure he was able to form those bonds. Besides, Elena worked for someone he would cut open, gut, and stake out. After seeing that happen, there was no way the woman would want anything to do with him.

"Good. I won't bother you any longer. I love you, Max." He blinked and jumped back into the conversation.

"Love you, too." He smiled and opened his eyes. "May I talk to Dad for a second?"

"Okay, here he is."

He heard his dad kiss his mom before answering, "What's up?"

"Thanks for taking care of that for me. I'll do better." He did tend to forget to check in with his mom, which caused issues.

"No problem. Everything going as planned?"

"A bit faster than planned, but now, it's a cat-and-mouse game. I've baited the hook, but I'm not going to set it until I know I'll have access to the big fish."

"I have every faith you'll do what you need to," his father said. "I'm outside now, and Mom is inside. Is there anything you need from us?"

"No. I have everything I need."

"If you need assistance …"

"You know I won't. I have three fucking shadows to watch my six. Don't you dare show up here."

His father sighed, "I know, but I'll be there in a heartbeat if you need me."

"Thanks, Dad. I love you."

"Right back atcha, kiddo. Be safe."

Max disconnected and flicked his screen back to his current target. The weakest link. He'd use the woman to get close to Abrasha, and then he'd kill the bastard and anyone who tried to get in his way. Val, Malice, Reaper, and Val's husband, Smith, were making their way to their hotels.

He watched as Elena flopped her thick, brown hair over her shoulder and read an article. One he'd supplemented without the publication's knowledge. His program had suggested numerous places to sprinkle his false persona, and he'd chosen a couple of other magazines to sprinkle with his newfound expertise.

He watched as she thoroughly searched for anything mentioning him on the web. That meant Abrasha could access her searches, too. Given she'd worked for him for the last four years, he wasn't sure if the man would, but he wouldn't take anything for granted. She had quick intelligence and knew her art—or at least that was his current perception at that point. In the future, his initial analysis could and probably would change.

With step one accomplished much sooner than anticipated, he would wait to make contact when she reached out to him with Abrasha's bona fides. Rushing wouldn't fit the plan he'd carefully constructed. Strangely, that bothered him. Like one mistake in a line of code that led to finding many others. It was a detail he couldn't abide by, but it was there, and he needed to find out how far it went and exactly what it affected. Regardless, either before the show Elena was planning or after it, Abrasha would cease his reign of terror.

CHAPTER 4

Maximus knocked on the hotel door after ensuring he wasn't followed or tracked. A massive man resembling a younger, stronger version of Abrasha Molchalin answered the door. He uttered one word. "Maximus."

Maximus gave his passcode, "Force."

The man opened the door, revealing a forty-five in his hand, and ushered him in. "Val, Malice, and Reaper are in the kitchen. I'll make myself scarce."

"Why?" Maximus turned to look at the man. "My plans include you."

"Excuse me?" Val said as she walked out of the kitchen with a glass of wine. "He's still recovering from surgery."

"Can he talk for himself?" Maximus asked and

turned back to Smith. "I think you at the show would cause enough of a diversion and commotion with the guards that all of us would benefit."

Smith crossed his arms over his chest. "I would like to know your plan before I agree."

Max smiled. "I like him." He jabbed his thumb at Smith while talking to Val.

"Yeah, well, I have you beat. I love him." She went over and leaned against the wall of muscle as he protectively put his arm around one of the deadliest women in the world.

"Max, I'd say it's been a long time, but then again, that would be an understatement," Reaper said as he and Malice walked out of the kitchen. Malice had a sandwich, and Reaper had a drink in his hand. "Can I get you a drink?"

"No, thank you. I don't drink."

"Yeah, why's that?" Malice asked.

"My mother doesn't like the smell, and I never acquired a taste for it." Max shrugged. Reaper chuckled. "Mommy issues?"

"Man, if you knew my mom, you'd have them, too. Are we ready to get down to business?" Max sat down in the chair nearest to him.

"Always," Malice said. "What's the plan?"

Max shrugged. "Killing Abrasha in a very loud,

very public fashion." He glanced at Smith. "Will that be an issue with you?"

Smith sat down on the couch with Val and leveled a stare at him. "Only if you fail."

Max smiled at the man. "That won't happen this time. All right. This is what I've worked out. Elena Ivanova is his art curator. I have an in with her. At this point, I have nothing indicating she's in bed with Abrasha, but she's worked with him for four years."

Reaper whistled. "And she's not dead?"

"Are you sure she's not his mistress?" Val asked.

"From everything I've discovered, she's a permanent resident of Sochi, and there's nothing to indicate a relationship other than through art." Max shrugged. "You can have Con or Jewell dig if you want, but they'll find the same thing."

"Oh, that's right, I forgot you were good with computers, too," Malice said with his mouth full of his last bite of sandwich.

"I know a thing or two," Max acknowledged. They'd never know how good he was. No one would. "She's planning two showings. One in two weeks, the next two weeks after that. She doesn't know about the second showing."

Smith narrowed his eyes. "Explain that, please."

"I've enticed her with a ploy suggesting my clientele is selling a highly sought after painting. She's sent Abrasha's financials, all verified by Swiss banking protocols. I won't make contact with her for a couple of days."

"Letting her stew," Reaper said, nodding.

"Exactly. Then I'll casually run into her." Max leaned forward and detailed the rest of his plan.

Smith looked at Val and nodded. She turned to him. "It has a lot of moving parts, but damn, I think you've got a good trap set up. The only thing I require is Smith to wear body armor."

Smith rolled his eyes. "That would limit my ability to fight."

She made a sound in her throat, and Malice leaned away from her. "Smith, your woman is growling."

Val reached out and punched Malice in the arm. "Shut up, brat."

With a laugh, Malice got off the couch. "I'm grabbing something to drink. Don't discuss anything important until I get back."

"Then hurry up!" Val yelled as he trotted into the kitchen.

Reaper leaned back and stared at his hands. "I can get behind the ploy. The identities will be solid?"

"Better than any you've ever had." Max smiled. "I guarantee it."

"And you're sure you can get the second showing?"

"No," Max admitted. "That's why we're setting up for support in case I have a chance at the target this weekend. But based on the intel I've obtained, I don't think Abrasha will be at the show then."

Malice returned with a bottle of water and a drink of some kind of dark liquor. He tossed the water to Max, who caught it and cracked the top. "What did I miss?" Malice asked.

"We're talking about setting up for plan B."

"As far as?" Mal sat down again.

"Why won't Abrasha be at the show? They're his paintings, right?" Smith asked.

"Again, you can confirm with Con and Jewell, but Abrasha isn't in Russia. We know he left last night. He landed in China and will be there for at *least* two weeks. It's a pattern he's established in the last two years. There's something or someone in China he visits every three months. He has the Chinese government's protection, but our satellites have been able to track him to a compound in the heart of the country owned by the Chinese government."

Malice's hand went to his ear, and then he chuckled. "Con wants to know how the fuck you knew that when he just got the information confirmed."

"Tell him he's too slow." Max smiled wickedly at Malice.

Malice started laughing. "I'm not going to repeat that, Con."

Val leaned forward. "Don't you have comms?"

"I do and will wear them during operations, but not in between. I won't be monitored. It's in my contract."

"Wait, what?" Reaper perked up. "You have a contract?"

"Hell, no." Max laughed. "I'm just a rebel."

"Well, that, I can respect." Reaper shrugged his shoulder and relaxed back in his chair.

"So, spill the beans and tell us what you want us to do or where you want us to be the night of the first showing." Val took a drink of her wine. "Some of us are still jet lagged."

"All right. So, we know the location of the venue. The Krasnaya Polyana resort. It's in the mountains not far from here." Max leaned forward and pulled a hand-sketched map out of his coat pocket. Everyone leaned forward to see the depiction as Max explained what he wanted.

"That's not much fun," Mal said.

"As I said, I don't think he'll be there."

"He has two weeks to return to the country," Smith said.

"Which is why Con and Jewell are going to try to track him," Max said.

"No, Con, I'm not telling him that either." Reaper chuckled along with everyone else.

"You can make plans for the second showing," Max said and stood up. "I'll be in contact."

"Don't be a stranger," Mal said, following him to the door.

Max chuckled. "You can bet on it."

"Which? That you will or won't be a stranger?" Val called from the living room.

"Yes." Maximus laughed and walked out the door.

Malice followed him out. "Yo, Max." Max turned and looked at the assassin. "I've got your back." He held up his hand, stopping Max's comeback. "Don't. I know somewhere out there, you have people who care about you, or maybe you care about someone. I know you'll do your job here and send a message. You're just as good at this as we are, but you don't work as often as we do. That, I know, is a fact. Yeah, you have skills we don't know about, and that's cool, but ... everyone, even the lone wolf, still needs the pack occasionally. We're here. Understand?"

Maximus smiled. "Momma Mal. I get why they call you that now."

Malice rolled his eyes. "So, fucking sue me. My people matter; even though we don't interact much, you're still my people."

Maximus turned and extended his hand. Malice grabbed it. "Whatever it takes, brother."

Malice smiled. "As long as it takes."

Maximus turned and walked away. Yeah, he was a lone wolf. He preferred the quiet to any effort at peopling. But Malice was right. He had a family he cared for and people who cared for him. He wasn't a fool; he'd call in backup if needed. But the takedown was his. The message that needed to be sent was his to send. Abrasha had had his time. Well, he'd fucked around, and now, it was time for him to find out.

CHAPTER 5

Maximus strolled through the impressive private art gallery on the banks of the Black Sea. There were a few artists displayed who showed potential. He stood staring at an abstract on black canvas. The dark reds and oranges mixed with whites and yellows showed depth and consideration. The blocking or positioning of the center of the work was off, making it less pleasing to the eye's natural tendency to put the painting into proportion.

"Fancy meeting you here." Elena's voice behind him didn't surprise him. He knew she was going to be there. Turning to look at her, he pretended to be confused. "I'm sorry, you're …?"

She smiled tightly. "Elena Ivanova, we met at dinner a few nights ago."

Max blinked and then smiled. "Of course, excuse my lack of memory. I've been extremely busy. Today has been the first day I've been able to get away from paperwork."

Elena nodded. "I left a message that I'd submitted the information you requested about the artwork we discussed."

Max nodded. "Oh, yes, well, the people I represent are still debating the timing of that sale." He turned to look at the abstract on the wall. He needed to establish a connection with this woman, and he could do it through the art in the gallery. "This one shows promise, but …"

"They need to refine the placement. The colors are resplendent and calming even though they're so vibrant."

"Calming?" He turned and stared at the painting. He stood beside her as they gazed at the picture, and he realized it wasn't the *painting* that was calming; it was her presence that seemed to give off that vibe. Again, a detail he needed to follow and find out why it was happening. The woman's presence was a mental computation with several of the factors missing. That made him smile. He loved a challenge.

Focusing on the painting again, he cocked his head to try to find the sense of calm she saw. If he were honest, the painting looked like someone in a rage had splattered the paint against the canvas and then let it dry. Abstract would never be his thing, but he understood it now that he'd studied the mediums and styles.

She made a sound of agreement. "To me, it's a sunset or perhaps a sunrise, illuminating and warming." She stood beside him and stared at the painting.

Max turned and smiled at her. "You're an optimist."

She chuckled. "Guilty. I take it you're not?"

"I see anger and power in the strokes and flow. The lack of discipline in the positioning is probably a rebellion by the artist." He walked three feet over. "And this? What do you make of it?" He pointed to a seascape. The waves crashed against a cliff face, and the howling wind was perfectly depicted.

She glanced from one painting to the other and whispered, "I would have never placed these two paintings together."

He nodded. "It shows a lack of respect for the styles. The hyperrealism of this painting suffers beside the abstract and should be displayed against a single wall, not in conjunction with different styles."

"A rookie mistake," Elena agreed. She glanced around. "The owner of this gallery has recently changed. The quality of the shows has started to slip."

"But what do you think of the painting?"

She leaned forward and examined it for about two minutes before turning to look at him. "It …" She shook her head and looked around before leaning toward him. "I believe this is a hand embellished giclée. It isn't original."

"I agree." Max made a motion to the painting. "That would never have made it past my line supervisor, let alone be placed in a showing."

She made a sound of agreement. "Unfortunately, some acquisitions are beyond a curator's authority. I have several my client purchased that I hide and pray never see the light of day."

Max pulled a face. "That bad?" Her eyes widened comically, and he laughed at her. "Enough said."

"You know, I have a showing coming up soon. I've rented out the Krasnaya Polyana resort. The showing is by invitation only. If you'd like to attend, it could be arranged."

Max cocked his head. "When?" He looked at his phone and made a show of sliding to the calendar app, which he'd preloaded with events and meetings that didn't exist. She pointed to the weekend in question. He lifted his hand to his face and scrubbed the side of it as he sighed, looking at the app. "Does the show go on all weekend?" He looked up at her as he asked, making sure she knew how busy his cover was and that he was trying to work her into his schedule.

"Yes, it's a holiday of sorts for my employer. Each night, we'll display a different portion of his holdings."

Max frowned. "You'll be incredibly busy. Are you sure you want me there?"

Her blush was obvious. "I have many people coming. Besides, I have it all laid out. Of course, there will be problems; there always are, and if my employer wants a specific painting shown at the last minute, that can cause headaches."

"Your employer is that impulsive?" He shook his head as he messed with his calendar.

"He is …" Max glanced up as Elena chose her words. "Demanding as most powerful people are."

Max cocked his head, dropping his phone. "He hasn't …. No, that's none of my business." He brought the phone back up and messed with the app.

"What? What were you going to say?" Elena asked, clearly confused.

"He hasn't abused his position, has he?" Max frowned. "I've known many rich and powerful people who believe having money grants them certain privileges." He looked at her until what he was implying registered.

She put her hand to her chest. "Oh, no. He's never been inappropriate. He has a temper, but he's never treated me improperly."

"Well, that's a relief. I hate people who assume wealth and privilege give them the right to take from people who have less than they have." Max sighed.

"I don't have that type of relationship with him. I can count on my two hands how many times I've seen him in person. The last time was just not long ago when we received some new art. He's rarely in public, and security must be maintained for people of his importance, as I'm sure you know."

"I'm well aware," he agreed and nodded his head. "Yes, I can attend, and I'd like to see your collection."

"My employer's collection." She smiled at him.

"True, but I assume you manage, catalog, monitor, purchase, and deaccession."

"At a minimum. Don't forget conservation and restoration." She walked with him along the long corridor of paintings until they stopped in front of the next painting.

"Restoration is a demanding and precise niche. I'm not aware of any reputable restorationists in Russia."

"Ah, true, none working privately, but the State museum does have an easel restorationist who's very good. We've occasionally secured her services by greasing the palms of the government machine. I've had her work graded, and according to my insurance brokers, it's exceptional."

They moved on to the next painting, and Max stared at the canvas as he asked, "I don't mean to seem too forward, but would you be willing to join me for dinner? It's been many months since I've had the pleasure of company who could tell the difference between a giclée and understand the minutia of placement in a gallery."

"Minutia? Oh, you didn't just say that." Elena gasped and batted her eyelashes. "I spend *months* determining where a painting will show and at what angle and with what lighting."

Max laughed at the staged look of pain on the woman's face. "Perhaps I should have said nuances of placement."

"That's a much better statement, and thank you, yes. I'd enjoy having dinner with you." They spent the next three hours examining every painting.

What Max hadn't learned from his studies, he learned from Elena during their discussions. Of course, he made a mental note of what she said and would validate the knowledge or, if need be, correct her when he'd checked for accuracy. Politely, of course. She was sharp-witted, quick to understand his dry humor, and just as critical of the art as he thought she would be, although she found something in each painting to compliment. That was the artist in her—the understanding of the effort to place brush to canvas and show the world your mind's vision. As they talked, he absorbed the sense of calm that radiated around her. He took protective actions to ensure she wasn't crowded and the heat he felt being so close to her. Each factor was entered into the computation she was giving him, and still, there was no answer as to why he was so interested in her. With each passing conversation, he could feel an attraction forming. Examining it didn't yield any fruit. For the first time, he was stumped. It wouldn't last long, but the anomaly was curious and a bit exciting.

"Where would you like to dine?" Elena asked as they finished the exhibit.

He shook his head. "I have no idea. I'm afraid I've

been ordering in from the restaurant in my hotel. Do you have a suggestion?"

Elena considered the question before pulling out her phone and calling. She asked in fluent Russian, "Tosh, do you have a table tonight?" She shook her head. "No. Not for him. For me and an acquaintance." She smiled and thanked the person on the other end. "We have a table at a beautiful little seaside restaurant. The balcony has heaters so we can listen to the sea as we dine."

"That sounds perfect. Shall I call my car?"

She laughed. "No, it isn't far. We can walk." They gathered their coats from the check station at the entrance to the gallery. She placed her matching cape over her shoulders.

He helped her and then shrugged into his coat. "In America, nobody walks. A block or three, it doesn't matter."

She stopped and turned to him. A look of fear in her eyes. "Did you want a car? I didn't mean to assume."

He shook his head and took her elbow, turning her in the direction she'd been walking. "No, no, this is fine. Just a difference in lifestyles."

"That is true. Here in Sochi, the pace is much slower than in London or Moscow."

"You've lived in both places?" He held her elbow as she navigated some loose cobblestones.

"Thank you, and yes. My mom is British, and we have an apartment in London. I stayed there with her while I attended school after my parents divorced. My father works for the State museum, which is where I developed my love for art. He's just an administrator with no knowledge of the pedigree of the exhibits, but he has an eye for beauty."

"I thought State employees didn't make a lot of money."

"He doesn't. Why?"

"How can he support your mother in another country?"

"Oh, he doesn't. My mother's family was very well off and left her a sizable inheritance that she's kept in her name, so the State has no access to it. She isn't a Russian citizen, so she travels here for short visits to see me during my slow times. As I said, my father and mother are no longer married, but they're friendly and have always worked to raise me together. I was born in Russia and have dual British citizenship." She looked at him and laughed. "And I just spilled my life's story to you in one breath. I'm sure that bored you to tears."

"Not at all." He took her elbow again as they

stepped off the curb to cross the street. "I'll give you tit for tat. I was adopted and raised as the oldest of five. There's an age gap between myself and my oldest brother. I was considered gifted and studied in numerous fields before landing in the art world. A friend suggested I work in this field, actually."

"So, you didn't grow up knowing what you wanted to study?" she asked as they stepped up onto the sidewalk.

"It's my understanding my brain works differently from other people. When I was younger, some said I was developmentally challenged."

She gasped. "No, they didn't. How could they? Your knowledge of the field is impeccable. I've read articles where they mention your work and insight."

Max smiled. "So, you've done your due diligence, Ms. Ivanova."

"Please call me Elena. I have, and I would be remiss for not reminding you I sent the bona fides for my employer should your owners decide to move regarding that painting." She stopped and sighed. "But that's not why I agreed to dinner with you. It's nice to talk to someone who understands what I say. Someone who knows the provenance of the masters and can talk to the state-of-the-art world today."

"I'll gladly take a look at those documents. As you know, I'm not the decision-maker in these instances, but I'll forward them to those who are."

Elena's face glowed with happiness. A niggling of guilt tickled at his gut. He was using the woman to reach the devil, and unfortunately for her, she was his only way forward. She motioned toward the door. "This is us, and honestly, that's all I could hope for. I haven't mentioned the possibility to my employer. I must let him know if he's found to be acceptable."

"That's entirely understandable," Max said as they entered the restaurant.

The hostess led them to a table on the balcony, and even with the gentle breeze, the ambiance was one of candlelight warmth and seclusion. Max held her chair for her before he seated himself.

"Would you like a drink?" he asked.

"I don't drink." She shrugged. "I've never acquired the taste."

Max smiled. "Nor have I." He placed the wine list to the side. "I've worked hard to keep in shape. Alcohol doesn't match that goal."

"Agreed. I exercise every day." She blushed and looked down. "I'll never be skinny; it isn't who I am, but I keep healthy by walking and yoga every morning. Curves are not currently in the hierarchy of the beauty world."

Max leaned over and whispered, "Then the world's view of beauty is wrong."

She glanced up at him and blushed beautifully in the candlelight. "You flatter me, and I thank you, but it isn't necessary."

"Perhaps you've forgotten the one truth in our business. Beauty is in the eye of the beholder. I think you are exquisite, and no, I'm not using my position to wiggle into your bed. The fact is you're beautiful to me." He leaned back. "You don't know your own value."

She shook her head and took a sip of water before answering. "I'm afraid I'll have to disagree with you." She changed the topic to the recent attack on the *Mona Lisa* at the Louvre. As they chatted about the audacity and entitlement of people today, he wondered who had hurt her. His research hadn't uncovered any long relationships or close ties with people in the area. He'd dive into her childhood that night. There was some reason for her belief that she wasn't beautiful.

They ordered, and she looked at him. "Where did you learn Russian?"

He made a face. "Why? Is it horrible?"

She laughed and shook her head. "No, very good, in fact."

"I must admit, I'm self-taught." Which was the truth. The best lies are those based on truth. Everything he'd told her about himself was a version of the truth. Keeping track of lies was a pain in the ass. Add to that the fact he found he didn't want to mislead her anymore, and the truth seemed to be the best way to go up to a point: such an anomaly, this woman.

"You must have a gift for language."

"As I said, many have said I'm gifted. If I put my mind to something, I can usually do it, at least with a modicum of success."

They talked as they ate. Max laughed at her jokes because they were funny, not out of duty. He found himself wishing he'd met Elena elsewhere, but then again, if he had, he wouldn't have approached her. She liked the person he'd become to take down Abrasha Molchalin, not the man he was. The woman wouldn't like a computer geek who killed because his sense of justice required him to do it.

They lingered over dessert before he leaned forward. "Do you suppose you'd like to go to dinner with me tomorrow night?"

Elena smiled brightly. "I'd love that."

"The café where we met?"

"That would be lovely. What time?"

"You're the one who has set hours. I work when I want and when required. What time would be best for you?" Max countered.

"Seven."

"Let me meet you, and we can walk to the café. I find I like that local custom." He put cash down for their dinner.

"I'm at the beginning of the promenade." She gave him the address of the office, which he knew, but hopefully, he'd be invited inside. He'd have a shot at installing a camera or two if she did.

"Then it's a date. But I must insist you let me call a car for you tonight. Walking home this late as a single woman isn't acceptable."

She shook her head. "I'm only a few blocks over. I've walked home much later, and there has never been a problem."

He frowned. "If you're positive, but I don't like it."

She smiled. "I've never had anyone worry about me getting home. It's an interesting feeling."

"It's called respect, and you should demand it." He got up and helped her out of her chair. After helping her put on her cape, he put on his coat, and they walked out of the restaurant. He stopped, took her hand in his, and bowed to kiss the back of it. He kept his eyes on her face as he did. Her shock was obvious, and then so was the blush. What wasn't as obvious was the zing of electricity that did a warp-speed lap through his body and crash-landed in his gut. He wanted to shout, *holy hell, what the fuck was that*, and ask her if she felt it, too. Instead, he smiled and said, "I'll see you tomorrow night at seven."

She smiled, slid her hand from his grasp, and turned to walk home. He watched until she reached the corner and looked back. She lifted a hand as she disappeared, and he did the same. Damn it, what was it about the woman that made him feel … what was it? Excited? No … eager. Eager to see her again, talk with her, and hear her laugh. That was an interesting turn of events. Another factor to add to the equation of who was Elena. He glanced at his watch and then headed back to his hotel. He'd have a nice long walk to work through the why's of the situation.

CHAPTER 6

*E*lena groaned at the sound of a truck backing into the delivery bay. She glanced at the clock. Fifteen minutes before Max would arrive, she had no idea what the delivery consisted of, which meant it was a purchase from her employer.

She carefully secured her office area, opened the rear door, and signed for the delivery. Thankful there was only one wooden crate, she waited while the driver placed the valuable merchandise into the back room. Her client's most expensive paintings were locked in the building's vaulted, fireproof areas. She needed to uncrate the item to determine where to store it.

Grabbing the battery-operated drill, she slid the battery pack into the machine, attached the appropriate screwdriver attachment, and started unscrewing the multitude of fasteners holding the front of the crate to the cross-arm-supported, standing base. She worked diligently until the chime from the front door rang, telling her Max was there. She dumped the screws from her hand onto the bench and walked to the front, still carrying the drill. After confirming it was Max, she hit the button, which unlocked the front door, and waited for him to enter the holding area. Once in and the front door locked, she buzzed him into the main office area. "You're right on time."

"And you're still ... building?" Max laughed and motioned to the drill in her hand.

"Uncrating a new arrival. I hope you don't mind, but I need to assess where to secure the painting before I leave for the night."

"Not at all. May I help?" He took off his suit coat and unfastened his cuff links as he asked.

"I can do it." She was instantly thrown off by the offer to help.

"I know you can, but why should you when I'm offering." He held out his hand for the drill, and befuddled, she handed it to him.

"Where is it?" He turned this way and that.

"Through that door. Follow me." She went through the process of letting them out of the office area into the delivery bay.

"Impressive packing," Max said and motioned to the characters that adorned the outside of the box.

"Chinese, I think."

Max knelt and started reversing out the screws she hadn't done. "Definitely Chinese. From Beijing." He pointed to a line of characters. "Handle with Care. Fragile."

He went back to the task of removing the crate's cover. Elena wondered if there was anything the man didn't know. When he'd removed the last one, she handed him a small crowbar, and he carefully pried the cover away from the base. He easily transported the heavy top to the far wall and leaned it there.

Elena carefully untaped and removed the plastic-covered sprayed foam wrapped around the painting. She knew Max came up behind her as she stared at the painting. It was another fake: new paint, canvas, not wood, no cracks from age, no dulling of the colors.

"Ah…"

She looked up to see Max rubbing the back of his neck. "You do realize that is..."

She sank back, sitting on her heels. "An unmitigated disaster."

"I was going to say fake, but yes, that, too. The original belongs to a Chinese billionaire."

She nodded and then sighed, probably more heavily than she should have. "I don't know why he does this."

"This has happened before?"

"Occasionally. I have a place for these, but I need to email my employer first."

"I can finish unpacking this for you while you send your email."

"You don't mind?" She wasn't worried in the slightest about leaving him alone with the painting. First, he was a foremost authority, and second, the painting wasn't worth the canvas someone had painted it on.

"Not at all." He turned to finish removing the foam packing.

"I'll be right back." She entered her code into the electronic lock and returned to the office. It took a moment to compose herself to send the email.

>>The delivery from China arrived today.

His response came immediately.

>>>>Put it with the others.

She sighed but sent another message back to him.

>>Then you are aware it is worthless?

The email pinged back seconds later.

>>>>It is not worthless to me. Store it with the others.

She acknowledged his instructions and signed out of the email system. When she returned to the delivery bay room, Max was casually leaning against the workbench with a befuddled look. He shook his head as she walked in.

"What?" she asked.

"I'm trying to find a logical reason for buying a fake." Max gestured to the painting leaning against the wall as he spoke.

"I have no idea, but he knew it was fake when he purchased it and sent it here. He just told me to store it with the others."

"Well, good, at least he answered. I worked through lunch, so my stomach thinks my throat has been cut."

Elena blinked and then laughed. "I haven't heard that saying in a long time."

"It's an accurate description for me today." Max

walked over to the painting and lifted it. "I think the frame is worth more than the painting."

"I don't doubt it. Are you sure you're okay to carry it? I have a cart." She pointed to the cart she normally used to transport the priceless paintings from the delivery bay to the vaults.

He picked it up and hefted it a couple of times. "It's far heavier than it looks, but I have it. Lead the way."

Elena took him back to the office area and another set of doors. That time, she shielded the keypad with her body as she entered the code. She also placed her finger on the pad and then used a fresh alcohol pad to wipe off her print, as Abrasha had taught her. The wrapper and pad were deposited into the trash bin beside the door. She spun the handle on the vault and then pulled the door open. Lights turned on and flooded the area. They traveled through the entry area, and she completed the same process to enter the back chambers. The fire suppression system, alarms, security monitors, humidity monitors, temperature controls, and the vault build made it one of Russia's most expensive and extensive systems. Artem Sokolov, Abrasha's head of security, monitored the systems remotely—redundancy to ensure the painting's security. Max walked in behind her and whistled. "Kahlo, Picasso, Cezanne, Van Gogh, da Vinci ... is that a Turner?" He held the painting he was carrying to the side, staring at the masterpieces hanging in their controlled environments.

"It is." She smiled. "Come on, this way." She led Max back to the small holding area off the main room with all the controls the other paintings were afforded, but the paintings were segregated. She pointed to a series of blank easels. "Over there. Any of the empty spots."

Max carefully set the painting down, which she appreciated. He looked at the others propped on easels and then back at her with the same befuddled expression. "Again, I have to ask, why?"

Elena laughed and shook her head. "I cannot speak for my employer, although I have told him all these are worthless."

"There are what ..." Max did a quick count. "Twelve here?"

"Thirteen. The first one he punched his fist through." She pointed to the empty frame that sat in the corner and shrugged. "I'm just glad it wasn't one of the good ones."

He swung around. "He'd do that?"

She smiled and shook her head. "I don't think so, but they're his property. Shall we?"

"Of course." Max smiled and exited the room. After she closed the door, he extended his elbow, and they strolled back through a portion of the most beautiful artwork in the world. "I would love to come back and admire the collection."

"After the showing, perhaps?" Elena suggested. "I'll be crating some of these for the show. You can come back and admire the ones my employer doesn't want at the show."

"That sounds like a deal, and I have a surprise for you." Max waited for her to secure the vault.

She turned around. "Really, what's that?"

"The people I represent have accepted your collector's bona fides."

Elena gasped and then hugged Max. "Thank you! I can't wait to message my employer."

Max laughed and hugged her tight against his hard body. She released him, but he held her for a second longer. The feeling of being possessed by the man should have made her wary, but she wasn't. She wanted that feeling. She wanted him to need and want her. "I'm sorry," she apologized, trying to recapture any modicum of professional demeanor.

"I'm just so excited. Meeting you was such a wonderful thing!"

"You can hug me anytime." Max smiled and winked at her. "Let's get some dinner."

"Yes, please." She locked up the facility and checked the alarm status and fire suppression systems to ensure they were active. She draped her cape around her shoulders, and Max opened the door for her. Her smile was so wide it hurt her cheeks. "This will make him so happy." She accepted Max's elbow and wound her hand around his arm. The solid, warm feeling of having a strong man towering next to her was curious and wonderful.

"What are your plans for the future? Will you remain a private curator for the rest of your life?"

Elena shook her head and chuckled. "I would love to find a position at a museum. I know that sounds like a large step down, but I would love to have a family someday, so I would need a position with normal hours. My father advised me not to take this one, but the money was too good. I've saved most of my wages, so I can take my time and find a good fit when my contract ends. What about you?"

"Oh, I won't stay in art much longer."

Shocked, she stopped walking and turned to look at him. "Why?"

"I'm better with computers than I am with people. While I now have a deeper appreciation for the beauty, history, and culture of art, I'm afraid my passion is actually with computer systems and code. There's a beauty in creating programs that can do things nothing else can." He shrugged and darted a glance at her. "Don't hate me for that."

"Hate you? Never. But I'm truly amazed at your immense and varied talents."

He chuckled. "I've built a system that takes the entire basement of my home in the United States. So, I think taking care of your employer may be my last foray into the lovely world of art."

"Really? That's amazing." They started walking again. "What's it like being that intelligent?"

Max threw back his head and laughed. "Intelligence should never be confused with smart. My father taught me that. Smart people use common sense, engage appropriately, and weigh the pros and cons of actions. Intelligence is only a factor of being well rounded."

She smiled at him. He was probably the most handsome man she'd ever been that close to, and even his cologne invaded her senses. "I think the art world will miss you."

He patted her hand that rested on his arm. "I am

but an insignificant ripple on the surface of a multitude of tears shed by the masters of the past and present."

She looked over at him. "And you are a poet. If you keep that up, Mr. Stryker, I may become enamored."

He smiled at her and stopped walking. He was so close. His arms circled her, and he whispered, "Shall I quote Elliot, Neruda, Atwood, or Whitman? I will do whatever it takes to keep you close to me."

Her heart pounded so hard she swore he could hear the thing thundering. His eyes strayed down to her lips and then back up as if asking permission. She leaned forward just slightly and toed up. The instant his lips touched hers, a sigh formed, and she melted into his strong arms. The taste of the man was an exquisite explosion, so bright she could sense nothing but him. When he lifted away, she held her eyes closed for a long moment, praying when she opened them, she didn't see mocking laughter. She gripped his lapels and slowly looked at him. The intense gaze wasn't mean. It didn't mock or criticize.

His eyes narrowed. "Why were you afraid just now?"

She looked down and carefully smoothed the fabric her hands had rumpled. "That's a long story."

He kissed the top of her head and hugged her tighter. "I have all night, but I can wait until you feel safe enough with me to tell me."

"Thank you." A shiver ran through her.

"You're cold. Shall we go to the restaurant?"

She nodded, unable to tell him the shiver wasn't from the cold. Or was it? The memories of her one and only lover brought a horrible chill to the very center of her soul. His arm circled her waist as they walked. She searched for something to talk about other than memories that haunted her. She grasped at a thought. "Where do you live in America?"

"New York City." He glanced over at her. "Where do you want to move when you're no longer employed here?"

"Oh, I don't know. I've never visited America, but I've heard wonderful things about MoMA and the Guggenheim." She'd never thought of going to America before then, but seeing where Max lived had become a wish just that quickly.

"I've spent time recently in both. They're impressive, but there are private galleries that rival in quality. New York would be a place you could find your next position." He winked at her and smiled. "Unless I scare you off all of America, which would be a shame."

She chuckled. "Right now, there's no fear of that."

"But for a second you were." He reminded her of her reaction.

She sighed and nodded. "A very short, very bad relationship. I'm afraid it left a few mental scars."

Stopping outside the restaurant, he tipped her chin up with his finger. "A beautiful woman like you shouldn't have scars."

She smiled sadly. "A sweet sentiment, and yet life does tend to mark us, doesn't it?"

He nodded. "It does. Shall we?" He nodded to the café's door.

"Yes, please." They entered and were shown to her usual table. Her tea and an extra cup for Max appeared. Marissa took their order and left them to visit.

"So, tell me about the show. Are you ready?"

"I am. I can't wait to introduce you to my employer. He'll be so excited when I email him tonight and tell him about the possibility of bidding on that painting." She felt giddy with excitement. It was a major accomplishment for her.

"Will you be too busy for dinner?" Max lifted an eyebrow as he poured their tea.

She smiled. "Too busy to eat? Never." She looked

down at herself. "As you can see, I rarely miss a meal."

"I see a woman with curves in just the right places. I don't see the attraction of a skeleton." He shrugged. "I understand everyone has their preferences. You are mine." His eyes met hers over their drinks.

She set her cup down and drew a deep breath before she asked, "Why?"

CHAPTER 7

"Why?" Max repeated the question. God, he wished he could put his finger on that exact answer, but he didn't have an answer other than ... "You intrigue me."

"How?"

Max leaned back and lifted an eyebrow. "Such hard questions for a second date."

Elena blinked and then laughed. "True. I'm sorry."

He smiled and leaned forward, covering her hand with his. The feel of the woman was addictive or could be if he let it. And God knew he wanted to let the addiction flow through his blood. He wanted to experience the woman and decode what script made her smile, what sequences made her who she was, and how the asshole in the past had injured her. He wanted to find that hanging bit of code and sweep it away so she couldn't remember the pain or the moments when she wasn't held in the most precious way. Whoever the woman chose in the future would be extremely lucky. Beauty and intelligence, or smarts, as his pops would say, were rare, especially when there was a physical reaction like he had with her. "So, tell me, if you had a magic wand, what would your life look like in ten years?"

Elena's eyes popped wide, and then she laughed. "I don't know that I've thought that far in advance. Someday, as I said, I'd like to have a family. A husband, maybe children, and a dog."

"A dog? Not a cat?" Max asked, surprised.

"No, why? Are you a cat person?" Elena asked.

"I'm not, but I thought all women loved cats." He frowned. His sister and mom sure did.

"That's lumping all women into a category. Would you do that with all paintings or all … computers?" She took a sip of tea as she watched him.

He frowned even harder and then made a face. "No, I wouldn't, and I'm not sure what led me to do that now. I guess that kiss must have short-circuited my brain a bit."

The blush on her cheeks grew deep, and she smiled. "It was very nice."

Max clutched his chest. "Nice? Oh, that's the death sentence of relationships."

Elena laughed, and so did he. He took another sip of his tea and almost choked when he saw Malice and Reaper walk into the café.

"Would you excuse me? I'll be right back," Max asked and wiped his mouth.

Elena's face fell. "Did I do something wrong?"

He settled back into his chair and put his hand on hers. "No. I want to obliterate the person who made you feel so insecure. I need to use the facilities."

She ducked her head. "Oh, sorry."

"There's nothing to be sorry about. I'll be right back." He lifted her hand and kissed the back of it before standing and making his way to the front of the café. Reaper looked up and saw him. He elbowed Malice, who frowned and glanced up from the menu he was reading.

Max went into the bathroom and washed his hands. When he came back out, the Shadows were gone. He didn't need Elena to recognize either of the men. They enjoyed their dinner and talked of nothing of consequence, but the conversation never dulled. He enjoyed the way her brain worked. She wasn't predictable, and he didn't get bored talking to her. He was mentally present at all times like he was with his family. The connection he'd made with her was rare.

When they left the café, Max paused on the sidewalk. "May I call you a car tonight?"

She smiled and shook her head. "I walk home every night. Sochi is safe, the promenade is well-lit, and people here walk everywhere. Thank you for asking."

"Some night, you'll allow me to see you home safely." He reached into his pocket and pulled out a business card, not the metal card he'd given her when they first met. "This is my cell phone number. Please call me when you get home."

Taking the card, she put it in her pocket. "I will."

"Dinner tomorrow?" As he put his hands on her hips, her soft form charged the electric bolt he knew would land in his gut and linger far past when she left.

"I'd like that, but let me call you with the time. The preparation for the show has started to turn, and I'm not sure when the workers consigned to re-foam the crates will be done."

"Then I'll say goodnight." He lowered for a kiss, and yes, that bolt of electricity damn near jolted him to the moon. He teased her lips with his tongue, and she folded into his embrace, opening for him. The taste of her filled his senses, morphing that bolt of electricity into a nuclear power plant sucker punch to the gut. He wasn't the one to move away first that time. She pressed her hands against his chest lightly, and he groaned, hating the thought of leaving the amazing deliciousness of her kiss. He relented and dropped his forehead against hers. "Dear God, tell me you feel what's happening here."

"Feel it? Oh, yes. I feel it. I do." She moved and looked up at him. "Maybe tomorrow night you can walk me home?"

Max stared at her. "Please don't play with me, Elena. I'm on foreign ground here." Hell, he was in the wilds of an uncharted universe's vast cosmic ocean. What was happening now wasn't foreign; it was impossible, yet there he was—lost without an anchor to stop his star and hers from colliding.

She nodded. "So am I. Perhaps we can find a way forward together. Tomorrow night."

He dropped for a light taste of her before stepping back, trying to break whatever magic she'd cast over him. "Call me when you get home."

She nodded and bit her bottom lip, which did some crazy things to his already on-edge body. Then she smiled and turned, walking away from him. He watched until she turned and waved at a bend in the promenade that would take her from his view. He lifted his hand and turned around. He made it about thirty feet before laughing. "Can you be any more obvious?"

"I wasn't trying to hide," Mal said as he walked out of the shadows. "This is why we need you to wear your comm device."

"What? A run-in at the café? I think we managed just fine without comm devices." Max glanced at Malice.

"Avoidable if we'd known you were there, and Con could have told us." Mal made his point again.

"I'm not going to have Con in my ear, but I've something for him to run to the ground."

Mal chuckled. "I, like Reaper, refuse to repeat those things, Con."

Maximus chuckled. "Abrasha shipped a painting from China. It's a horrible knockoff of a painting in a private collection. Con, find out if there's an influx or outpour of money."

Mal frowned. "You think he's laundering money?"

"Maybe, but then … no. No, that painting was heavy. I mean, too heavy. I tried to get into the back of the frame, but I couldn't without damaging the exterior, and Elena would know I was looking for something. And there are twelve more paintings with the same type of heavy frame." The thirteenth frame was in the vault on the floor.

"Smuggling," Malice said.

"Yeah, but *what*, and why smuggle anything *into* Russia?" Malice stopped and looked around to make sure they were alone. "You know what we believe he was doing and the operations to take out his launch capability?"

"I'm aware, but no radiation was coming from the frame, so I'm not concerned he's importing uranium." Maximus stared at his coworker.

"How do you know that? Con, stop. I just asked that." Malice rolled his eyes.

"Easy." Max lifted his suit jacket, pushed the middle post of his watch, and the dial flashed to a meter. "It detects any radiation."

"Wow, that's some super-spy shit, right there." Malice reached up and pulled his earpiece out of his ear. "Dude, I get what you mean. Con in your ear can get a bit hectic. Okay, so if you don't think it's nuclear, what do you think he's smuggling into the country?"

"I don't know, but I know how to find out."

"Open one of the frames. How secure is that building?"

Maximus shook his head. "I think Merlin could get in and out without being detected if he's careful, but it will be difficult."

"That sounds like a challenge he'd look forward to." Malice chuckled and then sighed. "So, how do we get in?"

"The night of the second showing. We send Merlin in. He goes in, finds out what's in those frames, and trips an alarm on the way out. We wait two minutes, and then we start the party."

"That sounds doable. Split the response forces. And if Abrasha shows up for the first show?"

"Then Merlin will have to plan the break-in after we kill Abrasha."

"And the woman?" Mal asked as they started to walk again.

"What about her?" Max growled.

"Not judging, dude. I fell in love with my wife on a mission. I know it happens. Just be sure she's on our side. Having people question that premise sucks, by the way."

"I can imagine. I'm … I'm not a ladies' man. But this woman, there's something …" He shook his head and shut up. That kiss had rattled his brain more than he thought. He never shared his feelings with anyone.

"Yeah, I totally get that. Her voice or a special look turns you into goo on the floor. I so get that."

Max didn't say anything for a while as they walked. Then he remembered the three cameras he put into Elena's workspaces. "I've got eyes on her workspace, so I can tell if there's any movement on the questionable frames. Elena isn't complicit. That, I know for a fact. She despises the fake art and hates that it's locked up with true masterpieces. She invited me back after the show to view the paintings in the collection. I'll see what I can find out then, too."

Malice was quiet for a moment. "How are you going to bring her out of this mission?"

Max stopped and stared at the sidewalk. "I'm not sure she'd go if I had an out. I don't know if what we have is enough."

Mal rubbed the back of his neck. "Don't waste the opportunity. People like us don't get much of a chance to find the one, you know?"

"Not really. No." Maximus looked at his fellow Shadow. "If she could forgive me for lying to her, could she forgive me for killing?"

"Does she need to know about the killing? We

can shield her. The lying, my man, that would be on you." Mal slapped him on the back. "Think about it." He put his earpiece back in and started laughing. "Con, would you please shut up?" Mal rolled his eyes again and walked away from him.

Maximus smiled and turned in the other direction, returning to his hotel. He hoped he wouldn't return to the hotel tomorrow night, at least not until much later.

CHAPTER 8

*E*lena typed an email to her boss as she floated home. Her feet may have hit the pavement, but she wasn't aware of it. The new feeling that flooded her was what helped her levitate home. She tucked into the soft neck of her cape and smiled. Max Stryker was unbelievably attractive, and he wanted her. For how long? She didn't know, and maybe she was kiss-drunk. Maybe the dopamine flooding her system made her less cautious, but even a single night with the man was worth the risk. She couldn't see Max treating her the way Andre had. Andre was a chameleon who turned into a snake. He treated her horribly. She knew what he was doing, and still … A St. Petersburg State College professor pulled her aside and told her to walk away from the man, that he wouldn't stop demeaning her. He'd groomed others the way he was trying to condition Elena, and if she followed suit, she'd wake up in another country.

The fact that the professor warned her allowed her to escape that ending, and she never looked back. That same professor became her mentor; the woman was amazing and someone even Andre and his friends wouldn't cross. She was also how Elena met Abrasha. Her professor had recommended Elena for the curator position despite her lack of experience. Abrasha had hired her, and the rest, as they said, was history. Or it was until that night. Andre's ghost had popped up and almost ruined a spectacular moment. Max's kiss. Oh, that wonderful kiss.

"Where have you been?"

Elena spun and then was pushed back against the wall outside her apartment. "Artem, what are you doing?"

"Bitch, who did you take into the office?"

"What?"

He kicked the door to her apartment open and threw her inside, slamming the door shut behind them. The door came off one of its hinges and scraped along the floor. Elena scurried toward the couch, but Artem lifted her off the floor by her hair. "What's his name?"

"Max Stryker! He's an acquisition agent with a client who owns a painting Abrasha wants."

A backhand caught her cheek, and a blossom of red painted her vision as she fell to the floor. He picked her up again and shoved a picture in front of her. The picture was of Max walking out of the front door of the office. "This man?"

She nodded, and blood dropped onto the picture from her bloody nose. "Yes. That's him. Max Stryker. He works for a prince in the Middle East who owns a painting Abrasha wants. On the way home, I emailed him from my phone and told him they'd accepted his bona fides. Let go of me, you fucking animal." The man let go of her hair, and she scurried away. She lifted from the floor and put her hand to her nose, catching the stream of falling blood. "He's going to kill you for this."

"Abrasha? As if."

Elena stared at the head of security. She wasn't talking about Abrasha. She was talking about Max. Why she knew it, she couldn't pinpoint, but she knew Max would go ballistic if anyone hurt her.

"Did you tell this man who you work for?"

She bared her teeth at the man in front of her,

and she could taste her blood. "No, that's not how private sales work. You know that as well as I do. When I show him what you've done ..." She wiped her hand on her shirt, leaving a dark smear of blood. Her mind clicked, and she barked out a harsh laugh. "Abrasha has warned you not to bother me in any way without his knowing. He's told me so. You are not to bother me."

Artem walked up to her and grabbed her around the neck. "If you mention this to Abrasha, I'll kill you. You got mugged. Do your job, bitch. If this man doesn't check out, I'll bury you in a shallow grave so the dogs can come clean your bones." Spittle hit her face, but she didn't stop staring at her attacker.

When she didn't flinch or back down, Artem squeezed her neck tighter and tighter. Black spots formed in front of her, and she struggled to pry his fingers away from her neck. She hit the floor and coughed, trying to gasp air into her lungs. A kick to her ribs sent her into the legs of the small table by the couch. She cried out in pain. He lifted her head by pulling her hair. "Say a word to Abrasha about this, and you will die."

She looked at him and shouted, "Not before you do!"

Artem walked over. The last thing she saw was the sole of his boot.

* * *

Maximus's feet pounded across the floor as he grabbed his earpiece and flew out of his hotel. He took the stairs and hit the comms. "I need backup at Elena's apartment. Some fucker just beat the shit out of her."

"Was it Abrasha?" Con's voice came over the earpiece.

"No." He didn't know who the fucker was, but he would find out.

"Is medical attention required?" Con asked.

"Not Russian. I'm heading there now. I'll assess." The picture of that fucker choking her until she went limp was acid-etched into his brain.

"I'm on my way," Reaper said.

"We're heading out." Val came across the comms.

"Meet you there." Malice's voice came in puffs as the man ran. Maximus flat-out sprinted out of the hotel. Each frantic step pushed him closer to the small apartment. He dodged small dogs and leaped over bicycles that cluttered the sidewalk near the promenade. Max threw open the door to the apartment complex and ran down the hall.

An older woman was stooped over Elena. She looked up, terrified, and spoke in Russian. "Some man hurt her."

"I know. She called me," Max replied as he leaned down over her. Blood caked around her nose. Her pulse was strong, and she was breathing through her mouth. He looked at the older woman. "I have friends coming to help. Would you please wait for them in the hall and direct them here?" His hands shook as he examined her.

"I can do that." The woman stood up slowly. "I heard the yelling. I can describe the man who left."

Max nodded as he positioned Elena so he could pick her up. "I'll ask for his description after I care for her."

The old woman fretfully twisted her hands together. "Do you want me to call the authorities?"

"No." Max stared at the woman. "I'll take care of this man."

She nodded. Her old eyes held a lifetime of experience with the Russian government. "This is good. The authorities would do nothing. I have medical supplies if you need them."

Max nodded. "I don't think I will, but thank you for your kindness."

"Elena is kind to me," the woman said matter-of-factly as she shuffled out the door.

Max carefully picked her up and made his way back to her bedroom. He heard Malice before he saw the man. "Back here," Max called when the door scraped against the floor.

Malice was at the door in an instant. "Motherfucker. Who did this? I'll get a washcloth."

"Thanks. Con, I'm going to send you a video. I want to know everything about the man who hurt her."

"You got it."

Max pulled out his phone and sent the clip from his app.

"Fuck," Con said after a few moments. "This guy needs to be taught a lesson."

"Yeah," Max said. He took the cloth from Mal, then dabbed at the dried blood and swore under his breath.

"The rest are here. We'll fix the door. Smith will keep a watch outside to make sure no one is watching us," Malice said from the doorway.

"Thanks. I need someone to go over and pretend to

take this guy's description from the old lady. She saw him, and she isn't calling the authorities." Max could see the fingerprints on her neck and the boot print on her cheek. The bastard would die a slow, painful death.

"On it." Mal left, and he heard high heels clicking down the hallway.

"Hey. Can I help?" Val said as she came into the bedroom. She hissed when she saw the damage. "Damn, Maximus, that bastard ..."

"His name is Artem Sokolov, and he's a real nasty bastard," Con said. "He was prior Federal Security Service and was kicked out for being too violent, if you can believe that."

"I'm looking at validation of that fact. Where does he live?" Max spit out the words.

Con paused before he said, "Dude, you can't go after him."

"Why the fuck not?"

"He's Molchalin's head of security," Con supplied.

Max's shoulders rose to his ears as he tempered the desire to scream. That itchy feeling he tried to avoid was crawling under his skin.

"If you take him out, it'll put Abrasha on alert." That was Smith's voice over the comms.

"I am aware," Maximus ground out.

"Smith isn't your enemy," Val said quietly, her hand landed on his shoulder.

"I know. I know." Max pushed Elena's dark hair away from her face. "I'll make sure the bastard never hurts anyone again."

"When the time is right." That was Malice.

"I don't need to be reminded what my priorities are." Right then, it was Elena. Then it was Abrasha. After that, he'd track down that bastard.

"Yeah, you do," Malice said from the doorway. "You care for her. Whether or not it's serious, you have feelings for her, and when she wakes up, we need to know what you're going to tell her about us and yourself."

Val made a noise of agreement. "She's going to want to know how you found out about her being attacked. You can't spin lies on this one."

Reaper agreed from the comms. "You'll have to give her some version of the truth. The question is, do you trust her? If not, we abort this mission and look for another way to get to Abrasha."

"My gut tells me to trust her," Max said as he traced the edge of the fingermarks on her neck.

"Then go with that," Val said. "She's awake."

Max's eyes flicked up to Elena's, which were

blinking open. "What happened?" She looked from Max to Val and then back to him, clearly confused.

"Someone beat you up," Max said to her, his fingers still touching her neck. He reached up, pulled his comm device out of his ear, and pocketed it. Connor the others were invited to that conversation. "He choked you."

Elena gasped and tried to sit up. She hissed, grabbed her head, and dropped back to the bed. "Artem Sokolov. He wanted to know who you were and why you were in the vault. Who is she?" Elena glanced at Val and then closed her eyes.

"She's a friend. She, her husband, and others came to help me help you."

Elena opened her eyes and stared at him. "You aren't making sense. How did you know Artem Solokov was here?"

"And that's my cue to leave." Val's hand landed on his shoulder. "Call us if you need us."

CHAPTER 9

*H*er head hurt, and her neck was sore, but what was more important was how Max looked at her. That was the look her father had given her when he'd told her the family dog had passed. "How did you know about him, Max?"

The woman gave her a small smile, then slipped out the door, shutting it behind her. "She's very beautiful."

"Is she?" Max said and shook his head. "I hadn't noticed."

Elena closed her eyes. "My head hurts. Please don't make fun of me or make me ask you again."

Max took her hand in his. "I'm not making fun of you. Val is a married woman who may be beautiful, but I don't care. She's a coworker and a friend. That's all." He sighed and said, "I'm not an art dealer."

She opened her eyes and stared at him. "You are. I've read articles, years old." She put her free hand against her cheek and hissed. "He kicked me in the face."

"I can see the pattern of his boot on your cheek," Max said and then cleared his throat. "Your boss is Abrasha Molchalin."

Elena's eyes popped open. Her neck seized when she tried to move too quickly. The pain shot a sharp dagger through her brain, and she winced and groaned. "I didn't tell you that."

"You didn't have to. My organization knows you've worked for him for the last four years. They sent me to get to him."

"Get to him? For art?" She was so confused. "I don't understand."

"No. I work for a global security entity. Abrasha Molchalin is a wanted criminal." Max's voice was steady, unlike hers.

She wanted to cry. In fact, she might be crying. Her cheeks were wet, but she was too sore to care. She closed her eyes again. "My father said he was not a good man."

"He's killed a multitude of people and caused the

death of countless others. People whose only offense was being in his way. His crimes are beyond any other living being on this planet." Max's thumb stroked the back of her hand. She was quiet for a moment before her brain started to patchwork what he was telling her together. So, he didn't have art to sell. He only wanted …

Dear God, no. He couldn't be trying to use her, could he? Was she nothing but a commodity, again? Was his affection an act? Had she fallen for yet another great actor but horrible person? She turned her head, wincing, but she wanted to know if she was right. "You're using me to get to him." She pulled her hand out of his.

"At first, I was," Max admitted. "Then, after we met, not so much."

"What does that even mean?" She rolled away from him. Her body ached, and she wanted to sleep, to wake up and have all of it be a bad dream.

His hand landed on her shoulder, and she was glad for the warmth and the comfort, even if he was a liar.

"It means I've never met anyone like you. You're funny, beautiful, witty, how you see art, the world, life … you're so special. I realized that almost immediately. You're different, and how I react to you is different. I don't have the correct parameters to explain why I clicked with you, but I know I do. I've tried to figure out how to bring you out when I'm done here. But I didn't know if you felt the same way."

"Parameters?" She closed her eyes. "So romantic."

"I know it isn't romantic. But then again, I'm struggling here. In real life, I'm a computer specialist. Remember I told you I wouldn't be in the art world much longer? I'll go back to sitting behind my computers."

She remembered. "How do you know so much about art?"

There was a long pause, so long she turned back over, audibly hissing at the effort. "How?"

He tapped his head. "I can become what or whoever I need to become. My intellect is said to be off the charts. If I need to become a specific entity, I study, learn the right language and information, and then I am ... transformed."

"That's what you meant when you said your Russian was self-taught?"

He nodded.

"How long did it take you to learn about art and to speak Russian?"

"I taught myself Russian when I was thirteen. It

took a week to master. To become an art expert, a month." He shrugged. "I'm not sorry for going after Abrasha. He's evil in its basic form, but I'm so sorry Sokolov attacked you because of me. I told you the truth whenever I told you how I felt about you. You matter to me." He shook his head. "Not many do."

"I need to think." She turned away from him.

"I understand. I'll leave."

"No!" She gasped in pain when she tried to grab him. "No, please, don't leave. Just give me time. I …" She looked at the door. "I don't want to be alone here."

Max looked at her. While his eyes were intense and angry, he touched her cheek gently. "You're safe. I won't let him or anyone else close to you. I'll be here until you tell me to leave." He stood up. "I do care about you, Elena. I didn't exaggerate that, nor did I lie about it."

She stared at him for a moment. "I believe you, but I'm… overwhelmed. Please give me some time."

He nodded and quietly left the room. She carefully moved to a semi-comfortable position and stared at the wall. She knew Abrasha was a powerful person. She understood the hesitation in people's eyes and knew that normal people didn't travel with five or six bodyguards. She'd buried her head in the dirt and built a life around the art she loved.

But at what cost? Was she enabling his cruelties? The paintings he bought for outrageous prices were worthless. Were they part of his crimes? She thought of the conversations she'd had with Abrasha. He was used to giving commands and expected people to follow them.

When she'd started working for him, Elena shivered as she thought of Abrasha's stern warning to Artem Sokolov. She'd overheard Abrasha threaten to kill him if he touched her without permission. The warning stuck with her for years. She always gave Sokolov a wide birth. That wasn't difficult on a daily basis. She only dealt with the man while transporting paintings to the showing venues. Tears streamed down her face, but she didn't care—her carefully constructed paper mâché world had crumbled. Sokolov's fists had destroyed it.

Her mind wandered to Max. Was that his real name? How did he expect to arrest Abrasha and extradite him from Russia? What type of political pressure did his global security company have? She doubted the Russian government would be pleased that he was in the country and stalking one of its billionaires, which put Max in danger. Her heart raced, beating hard against her ribs. If Sokolov investigated Max, would he find out who Max was? She'd given Sokolov Max's name. Oh, God … she had to warn him.

Elena carefully sat up and swallowed hard as she waited for the tiny fiend with a hammer and chisel inside her brain to stop bashing at her skull. Using the wall and furniture to support her, she shuffled into the bathroom and turned on the light.

Oh, God. The reflection staring back at her was horrid. Blood clotted in her nose, although it looked like someone had tried to clean her face. A waffle pattern from the bottom of Sokolov's boot was mottled red on her cheek. Her face was puffy, and the whites of her eyes were spotted with blood, but her neck … oh, her neck. She traced the finger marks that were clearly visible on her neck. She was lucky to be alive. The thought popped into her head, and she nodded slowly in agreement with her inner voice. She was very lucky Sokolov had stopped when he had. She'd never know why she'd taunted him when he was leaving. The comment was her truth, and she'd needed him to know it. She might die, but he'd die first. That was a fact she knew in the fabric of her being.

She washed her face using cold water, which felt

amazing against the heat of the bruising. After taking some pain relievers, she combed her hair and thought about what she would say to Max. How could she trust he'd told her the truth about his feelings for her? What proof could he provide? What proof did she want from him? Was that even a thing? Her mind batted all that away as she recalled she'd told Sokolov his name, and the chief of security would be searching for him.

It took far longer than it should have to change her shirt. Her neck and shoulders were so sore that moving them to shrug in and out of her clothes was an effort. She opened the bedroom door and used the wall for support as she went to the living room.

Max was in the kitchen, and he turned to look at her. "I've heated the water. Would you like some tea?"

"Yes, thank you." Elena moved to the chair and slowly sat down. Max had a cup in front of her by the time she'd adjusted enough to be somewhat comfortable. "I told Sokolov your name. You're in danger. He'll track you and try to confirm you are who you say you are."

Max sat down on the couch and leaned on his elbows as he looked at her. "Max is my real name.

Stryker isn't. My cover is unbreakable. He won't find anything except what I want him to find."

She reached for her tea, but he handed it to her before she moved too far. She wrapped her hands around the warm ceramic and stared at the liquid. "What's it like being you?" She wanted to understand. Her heart was begging her to find a way to live with the fact he'd used her as a means to an end. Even if his feelings were real, the fact he'd used her and continued his job remained.

He shook his head. "I'm not sure I know how to explain it. I am who I am. I've never known anything different."

"Your work for this agency. What exactly do you do?" She was grasping for anything she could hold as fact.

"Normally, I sit behind my computers and ensure things run as they should and bad actors don't infiltrate systems. I wanted to learn the art of this particular branch of service, so I convinced my superiors to let me train. I did, and I'm used on very rare occasions. To them, I'm more valuable behind the screens."

"But you're more important here in this situation. Why?" She sipped the warm tea and closed her eyes, letting the warmth soak through her.

When she opened them, Max was staring at her. "Because I could infiltrate the weakest link in Abrasha's closest set of associates."

It took her a few seconds to realize she was that link—the weakest of his associates. The thought stung, and she took another sip of her tea. "Was it always your thought to make me fall in love with you?"

Max blinked and cocked his head a little to the left. "What?"

"Do I need to repeat myself?" She was tired and in pain and didn't want to play that game.

"You've fallen in love with me?" Max asked, making the same movement with his head.

"What?" Elena jerked and hissed at the sudden movement. *She hadn't said that, had she?*

"You asked if my plan was always to make you fall in love with me. I'll answer that with as much emphasis as I can. The answer is no. I didn't believe there would be a connection between us for a second. I didn't because I've never felt this way about *any* woman. Connections are hard for me to form. Not because I'm autistic or have any physical or mental issues." He sighed and ran his hand through his dark hair. "I rarely meet anyone who can hold my attention. I know that sounds stupid, but except for my family, there are maybe four people in the world that I ... attend. I *listen* to their words instead of working on problems in my mind. I'm with them at all times. With you, *I'm present*. I'm here with you because of some connection I don't know how to define or recreate. I would if I could. I would make myself more normal and have a multitude of friends, but that isn't how my brain is wired." Reaching out, he placed his hand on her knee. "You asked me if I set out to make you fall in love with me. Have you?"

How did she answer that question? How did she explain? "I don't know how to answer that."

He looked down for a moment before lifting his eyes and saying, "Tell me what you feel."

She stared at him. "Betrayed. Scared. Hurt. Used."

"Fair enough," he said as his hand slipped from her knee.

She sighed. "If you'd asked me before Sokolov attacked me, I would have said yes."

"But now?" He reached forward and took her tea from her, setting it down on the table. Then he took her hands in his. "You knowing the truth about me, about why I'm here, doesn't change how I feel about you. But what do you feel for me now?"

She stared at their joined hands. Her emotions

were all over the place. "I suggest we wait and see." She saw his head cock slightly to the left and realized he made that movement when he got an answer he didn't anticipate. She clarified. "My feelings now are dominated by what happened tonight and what I learned about you and my employer."

"How would you like to go forward? I'll still go after Abrasha, but if you don't want to be a part of it, I'll find another way forward." Max still held her hands in his. Their knees touched. They were linked physically and emotionally. To what extent, she wasn't sure, at least not anymore.

"Is this the best chance of you arresting him?"

Max blinked. "This is the best chance we have now. It could take time to find another way."

"And you can prove he's guilty of these crimes you've said he committed?" She'd been sold a bill of goods and didn't want her employer unfairly persecuted.

He nodded. "I can get you the evidence. It's horrific, and it's absolutely true."

"I want to see the evidence. I want to confirm what you're telling me is the truth."

"And when I prove it is?"

"If you do, I'll help you." She watched to see if

she'd see any relief in his frame, but there was none. He only nodded.

"I'll have it for you when you wake up."

"You're leaving?" Her eyes darted to the door, which looked to be repaired to some degree.

"You asked me not to leave. I'll sleep on the couch. One of my coworkers will bring the information you need."

Relief flooded her body. He wasn't leaving. He'd be there if Sokolov came back. "I should take a shower and go to bed."

He stood up, still holding her hands. "Do you need help with anything?"

"Other than getting up out of this chair? No." A small smile played on her lips when his head cocked slightly to the left. His eyes softened, and he stood firm, helped her stand, and walked with her to the bedroom.

He lifted her hand to his lips and kissed the back before saying, "I'm here, and Sokolov cannot hurt you."

"You'd think he'd be the one I was concerned about hurting me, wouldn't you?" She saw him wince as if he'd been hit. Maybe she wanted him to feel a bit of what he'd done to her.

"I can't take back what happened. I can't make

that right. Nothing I do or say will change what I've done. But if you feel anything for me, judge me for what's happening now. My actions, not my words, can prove my intentions and character. Let them speak to you, not the wounds from your past."

She slid her hand out of his grasp. "Goodnight, Max." He smiled and turned back toward the living room. She shut the door and leaned her forehead against it. How could she feel so much for a man like him? A man who had used her and still wanted her help to reach her employer, a man who had only ever been fair with her. She'd need to be convinced Abrasha was the criminal they said he was.

CHAPTER 10

*R*eaper handed him a leather pouch. "I'll destroy that after you're done with it."

Maximus nodded. "Thanks." The information the pouch contained was not for public dissemination. However, to gain Elena's trust and help, he would provide a small portion of the evidence the Council had against him. The horrendous acts against humanity funded and perpetrated by Abrasha Molchalin were hard to read about, but she'd asked, and if he wanted to gain her trust, she needed to know.

"How is she?" Reaper asked from the doorway.

"Still sleeping." Maximus nodded toward the kitchen. "Tea?"

"I'm a coffee type of guy." The man smiled

momentarily before saying, "We'll be waiting, one way or the other."

Max knew what they'd be waiting for. Either they'd continue with the mission, albeit with restrictions on Elena's interaction with other people, or they'd escort Elena out of the country until they found a way to take Molchalin out. He hadn't told her that. That consideration wasn't in play at that point, but should she decline to help, she'd need to be protected, and by protecting her, it would protect him as he worked. It was a sucky solution, but one that would have to be addressed should she not be convinced by the evidence he'd give her.

"Thanks," Max said as Reaper turned to leave.

"Whatever it takes, my man."

"For as long as it takes," Max said as he shut the door and stared at the leather pouch. The information it contained proved Abrasha's guilt beyond any doubt. He heard the bedroom door open and turned around. Elena stood in a pair of yoga pants and a baggy sweatshirt. Her hair was a bit tousled, but her cheek was less swollen, and the red marks were lightened dramatically. The finger marks on her neck had darkened, which sent that familiar bolt of hatred through him. Itchiness that he couldn't scratch started to build, which wouldn't end well for Molchalin's security chief.

"Who was at the door?"

He lifted the leather pouch in his hand. "Delivery of the proof you requested." She walked across the room and extended her hand. "You might want to have breakfast before you look at that." She wouldn't be able to eat after she saw what was on those pages.

"I don't normally eat breakfast, but thank you." She kept her hand extended.

"Remember you asked for indisputable proof." After he handed it to her, he went into the kitchen and made her a cup of tea, taking it to her as she sat on the couch. Returning to the kitchen, he retrieved his cup, then sat on the other end of the sofa.

She pulled out the packet of papers and opened the file. He watched her expressions as she read the information. When she turned the page and saw the first picture, her hand flew to her mouth, and she gasped. "Oh my God." Her eyes popped up, searching for him. "Oh my God."

He nodded. "That's only the tip of the iceberg." He nodded to the pile of papers on her lap.

Her hand shook as she turned the photo over and read the next report. He sipped his tea and watched as she paled when she read the narrative. Flipping the paper, she saw the picture of Abrasha pointing a gun at a woman. The next photo showed the woman's brain exploding from her skull. Elena shook her head but kept reading. About halfway through the papers, she stopped and put the paperwork back together. She put all of it in the leather pouch and handed it to him. "I'll help you. He doesn't deserve to be a free man, and he needs to stand trial for the atrocities he's committed." He took the pouch and handed her the tea that had been steeping. She took out the leaves and set them on the small saucer.

"Why hasn't he been brought to justice?"

"He's very wealthy and travels with what constitutes a small army. Just when we think we have him, he slips away."

She took a sip of her tea. "But he won't expect anything at the show."

"He won't be at the show you're putting on." Max twisted his position on the couch to look at her and leaned back on the arm of the couch.

Elena frowned. "What do you mean?"

"He's out of the country, in China. When he makes these trips, he's always gone over two weeks. Has he ever missed his art showings before?"

She nodded. "Several times, which is always nice.

The guests seem to have a better time when he's not in attendance." She shivered and took a sip of her tea. "Now, I understand why."

"Instead of putting on two shows, can you push the date of this one back?" Max had an idea.

"I could, but what excuse would I give?"

"Being attacked."

Her eyes widened. "Well, it would be the truth."

"Exactly. Tell him you need time to recover and ask if he would be all right with pushing the date back by two weeks. That would give him time to complete whatever he's doing and return."

"Then you'll arrest him."

"Not me," Max said. "Arresting isn't my end of the stick."

"You just make it a possibility?"

"Yes. I do what is required to ensure the assignment is completed." He wasn't lying to her, but through omission, he wasn't telling her the truth either. That bothered him, yet another testimonial for the connection he'd somehow found with the beautiful woman.

"I'll email him and tell him about last night. Should I tell him it was Sokolov?" she asked as she stood up rather slowly.

"Would you tell him if I wasn't here?"

She stared at him for a moment. "Probably not. I'd wait for Abrasha to show up and then tell him. But I think Sokolov knows that, too. I think he'll threaten me again before Abrasha comes back."

"Then don't tell him yet. You don't need to worry about Sokolov. You'll never be unattended. I plan on being with you from now until the showing. If I have to leave you, as I do this morning, to shower and change, I'll make sure one of my coworkers is watching you."

She turned to look at him and winced, and he was next to her in an instant. "How are you feeling?"

"I've never been hit by an automobile, but I suspect if I ever were, it would be a close match to how I feel right now." She rolled her eyes. "Yes, I'm being a bit dramatic."

"You have every right."

"I'll go get ready for work."

"You're going to work?"

"I have to. There's a delivery from Abrasha's residence to the vault this afternoon. One of the paintings he wanted in the exhibit." She rubbed her arms. "You'll come with me, right?"

"Will that anger Sokolov?" God, he hoped it would. He hoped the man would show his face. He wanted three minutes with the bastard. Fuck that, he wanted three days.

"I told him what you'd told me, your name, your position, what we were working on. He will leave me alone if he can validate your identity as you said he could. He was never supposed to approach me. I heard Abrasha threaten him when I was first hired. I threw that in his face last night. He said if I told Abrasha what he'd done, I'd be dead. I told him he'd die first."

Max smiled. She had fight inside her. "That was baiting the bear, wasn't it?"

"It was stupid, actually." She reached up to his cheek. "It's why he kicked me."

Max touched the mark on her cheek. "Do you think Abrasha would kill his chief of security?"

"No. But I thought you would. That's why I said it. Was I wrong?"

"You weren't wrong." He *would* kill the man.

"He was in the pictures with Abrasha when he shot the woman. Sokolov is evil, too, isn't he?"

"He is, but I'm far more dangerous and skilled than he is. You're safe with me."

Elena stared at him for what seemed like years. Finally, she leaned forward and kissed his cheek. The simple touch was the sincerest action he'd ever experienced. It was pure, and he could see the embers of what had been in her eyes. He needed those embers to catch fire again. He'd move earth out of its orbit to ensure those eyes burned with the heat of a supernova again.

She blinked and whispered, "You won't let him hurt me again."

"Never." He helped her down the hall.

As she opened the door, she turned to him. "If I were to ask what you were going to do to arrest Sokolov or Abrasha, would you tell me the truth?"

"If you asked me, I would. Please don't ask." He needed her to know she could trust him, and being as truthful as he could be began that process.

"I won't. I think knowing wouldn't help." As she shut the door, a smile ticked the side of his lips. She had no idea how right she was.

He fished his comm device out of his pocket and put it in his ear. "Reaper."

"Oh, he's blessing us with his presence." Con sighed.

"Stop being a baby," Reaper said. "You need me, Max?"

"Retrieval. She's in, and she's going to work. I need someone to watch over her until I can change and return to her office."

"You got it. Be there in five minutes," Reaper acknowledged.

"Con, I've got eyes in the office. I'll send you access."

"What about the frames?" Malice asked.

"We'll find out today," Max replied and took a sip of his tea.

"What? What frames? How did you set up a camera system, and how do you know what I need to get into it?" Con rattled off the questions.

"Dude, he's a nerd just like you."

"Well, now, I'm really offended. No one's like me," Con said.

"I agree with that," Max said, pulling his earpiece out of his ear and shoving it in his pocket.

CHAPTER 11

*E*lena accepted Max's offer of a car ride to the office. Walking would be good for her sore muscles, but fear of Sokolov was a real and growing thing. Of course, she knew Max would try to protect her. She felt he was as dangerous as Sokolov, if not more so, yet the tendrils of fear kept lashing at her nerves. She'd jerked at her reflection in the mirror that morning. Stupid, yet it had happened. Now, pulling up to the office, her hands shook. She clenched them and tried to control her panicked breathing.

Max's hands covered hers. "I'll be with you. You can do this."

She nodded a bit, still too stiff to do more than that. "It's silly, but I can't stop being … jumpy."

"No. It isn't. If you didn't have some concerns, then I'd be worried. You're having the appropriate response based on the circumstances." He squeezed her hand gently. "Are you ready?"

She closed her eyes and tried to take a full breath before she said, "Yes."

Max opened the door and got out of the car. She took his hand and carefully slid out of the seat, letting him help her onto the sidewalk. The mint green silk scarf she'd wrapped around her neck hid most of the damage Sokolov had caused. The blood vessels in her eyes couldn't be corrected. The blood would take time to go away. Makeup covered the remaining redness on her cheek. She fumbled the security code twice before she could punch it in correctly. Max put the key in the lock. Her hands were shaking too much to do so. As she entered the office, the phone was ringing. She rushed over and picked up the receiver.

"Hello," she answered in Russian. Max pulled out a small box and set it on the vacant desk in the office. She frowned but didn't ask what it was.

"Elena. I just read your email. What happened?" Abrasha asked.

"I was attacked just outside my apartment. I'm … I'm very sore and shaken up. A neighbor scared the man away, but he was pretty rough. Could we postpone the showing for a week or two? I hate to ask, but ..."

Abrasha was dismissive. "Of course. I'll tell Sokolov to escort you to and from work. I will be directing him to find out who it was who attacked you. I will not tolerate an affront against one of my people. Sokolov will watch over you until we find this man."

"*No*, no, please don't do that. The art dealer I've been working with to get you access to that private sale is with me. We've become very good friends. If it's all right with you, he can work in the office with me since he'll be staying in town for the next month to conclude his business. Sokolov is too busy to babysit someone like me." She stared at Max as she spoke, and he nodded. *Thank God*. She hated lying and hated the fact her employer was a murderous bastard and his chief of security had viciously attacked her.

"I'm very pleased with your work on that point, Elena. You know how much I want that painting. You do continue to exceed my expectations. I will, of course, need this dealer checked out. I don't want anyone near my collection who hasn't been properly vetted."

"Yes, I understand. His name is Max Stryker. I'm sure you'll find his credentials to be impeccable. I did my due diligence." She smiled at Max, who had used that term.

"You seem to be quite enamored with him. I'm sure Sokolov's check will be thorough."

She let the comment about being enamored go but continued, "Thank you, sir. So, I'll push back the showing but keep it at the same venue. The manager of the Krasnaya Polyana shouldn't have a problem accommodating you."

"He better not," Abrasha stated matter-of-factly. Before that morning, Elena would have chalked up the tone of his comment to bravado, wealth, and privilege. Now, the threat was clear and present. She tried to laugh it off as she would any other time, but her laugh sounded brittle and forced. She prayed Abrasha would attribute any weirdness to her recent drama.

"I'll send you updates as I get them." She didn't want to talk to him any longer than necessary.

"Of course, you will. If you need anything, contact Sokolov. He can be there before anyone else."

"I'm sure Max can handle anything that comes up, and yes, I'll keep him in the office area until your checks come back and Sokolov tells me he's cleared."

"Good. I'm glad you weren't too badly injured, but I'm also not happy someone dared to attack a person who works for *me*."

"I think the man was a bit deranged." Sokolov was absolutely not thinking before he acted last night. That was a fact.

"That is not an excuse." Abrasha brushed her off. "Sokolov will find him. If not, I'll have the local officials work on it."

"Whatever you think is best." She shivered. "I just want to forget it ever happened."

Max's arm went around her, and she leaned into him.

Abrasha made a sound in his throat. "That is a woman's way of thinking. Letting this slide will not stop it from happening again. It must be stopped in its tracks."

She shivered at the menace she heard in his voice. "I'm sorry. It's just been a lot to deal with, to say the least."

Abrasha made a dismissive sound before saying, "I'll have Sokolov call when Mr. Stryker is cleared to enter the vault." The line went dead. She put the phone down and stared at him. He'd warned her not to say anything in the office because it was probably bugged. He'd said he'd check for electronic devices when he returned from the hotel.

"I should let you get changed."

"I'll be packing my bag and checking out of the hotel. I'm staying with you." Max wrapped his other arm around her, and God help her, she melted into his big, hard body. She wanted him with her. Not only because of what had happened last night but because of the feelings that had grown since she'd met him.

She sighed. "I should go to work. I have a lot of calls to make."

"I just placed a jamming device in the office—that box. No one will listen to what you're saying if there are bugs in there. Your desk phone will work, but your cell phone won't. It won't interfere with your internet connection. There'll be someone watching the building. You're safe. I promise."

She nodded. "I know. I trust you to protect me." She did. Only, no matter what her rational brain told her to believe, her raw nerves vibrated with tension, fear, and anxiety.

Max cocked his head to the left and then shook his head. "I'll be right back."

Elena sat down and watched as he left. As soon as

he was out of sight, she went to the front door, entered the code to activate the alarm, and locked the door. If Sokolov came to the door, it would take him time to enter, and she could lock herself in the delivery area. As far as she knew, he didn't have any codes for the interior of the building. Abrasha wanted two people to have the code: her and, of course, himself.

She huddled behind her computer and tried to stop shivering. It wasn't cold in the office, but still, she was freezing. Her world had turned on its head last night. The violence Sokolov had unleashed had stripped her of her sense of safety in a matter of minutes. She never wanted to feel that way again. She reached up and touched her neck. The bruises there were a reminder she could be dead. A whole-body shiver ran through those raw nerves, and she closed her eyes, praying tears wouldn't flow. No, she needed to be stronger than that. Max needed her help to take Abrasha and Sokolov into custody. She had no recourse except to be strong. Lifting her shoulders, she took a deep breath and then another. She powered up her computer and reached for her phone. She had calls to make and an event to push back. Sitting like a lump wouldn't get either done.

The office's familiar needs eased the stress, and

while she still glanced at the door anytime someone walked by, she'd made a dent in the items she needed to do and was feeling good about where she was when the phone rang. She answered and froze at Sokolov's voice. "Max Stryker is cleared."

She couldn't find her voice and didn't answer. The line went dead, and she dropped the phone onto the desktop. She pushed away from the desk, rolling her chair to the wall, staring at the phone. Her heart was beating hard against her ribs, and she started shaking again. No. No, she wouldn't let him affect her that way. She rolled her chair back to the desk, hung up the phone, and put her hands on her keyboard. The buzzer for the front door made her jump. She looked at the monitor, and relief flooded through her. She hit the buzzer to let Max in through the front door, and when it clicked shut, she went to the interior door and let him in.

She launched at him and wrapped her arms around him. His free arm went around her and held her tight. "What happened?"

"Nothing." She shook her head. "Well, that's not true. Sokolov called and told me you were clear."

"When did that happen?" he asked as he inched them into the office and shut the door behind him.

"Just now."

"Ah, that explains the shaking." He rocked a bit right and left as he held her.

She sighed and nodded. "I was doing so well until I heard his voice."

"That's understandable. The shock triggered the physical response."

She pulled away from him and looked up at him. "Did you become a psychiatrist once?" He smiled at her and winked. Her jaw dropped. "You did?"

"I may have been bored one summer." He shrugged.

She blinked and then laughed. "What is it like to be so smart?"

His smile fell. "It isn't what you'd think."

Reaching up, she slid her fingers along his cheek. "It's hard, isn't it? Having all that ability and keeping it all locked up."

He shook his head. "No, day to day, I'm with people who know what I can do. My parents were the ones who encouraged me to develop my interests. The people I work for know who and what I am. I'll take on a protégé when I get back, so there'll be someone else to talk with. I have to connect with a person not to tune them out. That sounds strange, but if someone bores me, my mind will flip to something interesting. I'm still attending the conversation, to a degree, but only enough to make it seem like I'm not blowing someone off. That took a long time to learn how to do."

She stepped back and waved to the spare desk in the office. "You can use this desk." She glanced down at the suitcase in his hand. "I'm sorry, put that anywhere."

"Thank you." He moved to the desk and put the suitcase behind it. Taking off his suit jacket, he rolled up his sleeves and loosened his tie. "What did Sokolov want?"

Elena's attention turned from his muscled forearms to his gorgeous face. How did she get so lucky? He stopped and cocked his head to the left. What had he asked? She couldn't recall it for the life of her. "I'm sorry, what?"

"What did Sokolov want?"

"Oh, he said you were cleared to go into the vault." She rolled her eyes heavenward. "I have a few more calls to make, then we can look at the paintings if you'd like."

He opened his suitcase and withdrew what looked like a computer from the Stone Age. "I'd like to look at the paintings in the storeroom."

She frowned as she sat down in her chair. "Why? They're atrocious. What's that?"

"And yet there has to be a reason he's shipping them to you and instructing you to keep them in the most secure vault in the city. This is my computer."

Elena pulled her bottom lip into her mouth and chewed on it as she silently agreed. But that computer ... "I thought you knew a lot about computers?"

Max stopped what he was doing and answered her, "I know everything there is to know about systems, programs, computer languages, algorithms, engineering, and applications. I'm learning artificial intelligence as it evolves. Why?"

She pointed to the block now sitting on his desk. "Then why don't you upgrade?"

He glanced down and then laughed. "If you had a choice between my computer or the one on your desk, which would you take?"

"Mine, of course." She wasn't a fool.

"That's why this computer looks like it does. It's rarely out of my possession, so the chance of someone taking it is almost nonexistent. Suppose a person was so desperate to take my ugly computer. In that case, it's safeguarded by bio-registries, additional fail-safes that would wipe its contents before someone could click a key, and a program that would spike any system connected to it."

"Spike?"

"Decimate it. Destroy it," he clarified.

"Oh." She turned back to her work. "That's pretty smart. Camouflaging a priceless computer in an ugly shell."

Max's head cocked to the left, and quick smile passed across his face. "Exactly."

CHAPTER 12

Max's mind shifted into overdrive as Elena worked. The painting he'd put into the storage room ... The specifications of the painting, approximate weight, canvas dimensions, and the frame ripped through his mind. The weight was off, and the frame was too thick, as were all the frames on the art that sat in that room. Whatever Abrasha was shipping into Russia was hidden in the frames or protected by the large frames ... He'd read cases of artwork being covered with newer paintings. It was necessary in the early ages when canvas for work was costly, and artists were among the poorest of the population.

"Max?"

He snapped his attention to Elena. "Yes?"

"Are you ready? I've finished what I can do today and sent emails to all parties pushing the showing back. I'll make calls to follow up with the guests who haven't RSVP'd to the date change, but it wasn't difficult to make the modifications. I think a lot of that cooperation has to do with Abrasha. Knowing what I know now, I can see why people bend for him."

Max nodded as he stood. "Does Sokolov have access to the office?"

"Yes, and the delivery area, but Abrasha and I are the only ones with access to the vault. If he showed up when you were away, I was going to hide in here." Elena moved toward the vault entrance. He picked up his computer and brought it with him. No sense in tempting fate.

He watched as she opened the small packet holding the alcohol wrap and went through the process of entering the vault and wiping the screen.

They walked through the hall of priceless art, art that should have been exhibited in a museum but was instead locked behind three-foot-thick concrete and biometric locks. He waited for her to open the storage room and headed straight for the frame in the corner without a painting. "What are you looking for?" Elena came over and watched as he kneeled on the floor and examined the back of the frame.

"Remember what you said about hiding something priceless under something ugly?" He glanced up at her.

"Yes." Her eyes widened. "You think something is hidden in the frame?"

He nodded. "Either the frame or under the painting of the canvas."

"An overpaint?" She dropped to her knees with him. "Why didn't I think of that?"

"Because until this morning, you assumed your boss wasn't a murderous bastard," Max said as he ran his fingertips around the outside of the frame.

"Well, there is that." She sighed. "What are you looking for?"

"Irregularities, dips, dents, color change."

She pointed to the right-hand corner. "There."

He zeroed in on the divot she'd pointed out. He ran his finger over the small indention. The texture was different from the rest of the frame. Sitting back on his heels, he stared at the composition of the frame. "This would need to open."

She nodded, sat on her butt, and crossed her legs. She took the frame from him and lifted it to the light. "There, a seam. You can see the color change in the wood finish." She handed the frame back to him. He lifted it in the same fashion she had and could detect the smallest change in color that ran in a straight line at the joint. He spun the frame to the opposite side and searched for the same tell-tale sign. "There," he said, and she pressed her face against his arm as he held the frame, squinting to see what he indicated.

"I see it, but what do we do now? If we open it, Abrasha will know."

"Not necessarily." He pulled out his phone and started taking pictures. He could get a replica of the frame in a day, maybe two. The weight, he'd have to take a wild-ass guess on unless … "Do you have a scale?"

"Scale? Yes, in the delivery area. When I have workers construct shipping boxes, I have to know how much they weigh to notify the company shipping the art its dimensions."

"Is it portable?" He reached into his pocket and pulled out his switchblade knife.

She backed away from the knife, her eyes wide. "I can roll it in here. What if he comes back?"

"I'll have a replacement built. He won't be able to tell the difference unless he looks for the lines and the divot." Max turned the frame over and then looked at the rest of the frames, leaning on easels. They were all different sizes and thicknesses, and some were an awkward fit for the canvas, overpowering the small paintings with height and girth.

He put the frame down. "Do you want help getting the scale?"

She glanced back in the direction of the vault door. "Would you mind? I can manage the scale, but …"

"Not at all." He stood up and offered her his hand. She was holding up pretty damn well, considering what she'd been through the night before. He left the frame and his computer in the vaulted area as he held her hand as they strolled back through the priceless treasures.

She drew a deep breath and let it out. "All of these were bought with blood money."

"Not necessarily. Abrasha's father was made rich by seizing an aluminum company in the early voucher campaign sponsored by the Russian government. From there, the man worked damn hard, and when he died, Abrasha took over. From what we determined, his father was a businessman and mostly worked within the confines of legalities. Abrasha took the businesses into the digital age and has gone for the easy money, backed the wrong people, and become a monster. Absolute power, in Molchalin's case, has corrupted absolutely."

She squeezed his hand. "Thank you."

He smiled, looking forward. She knew he was trying to make her feel better. He squeezed her hand and looked over at her. Not many people would have understood what he was trying to do. "For what?"

She chuckled. "You were trying to make me feel better about working for a murdering pig by telling me some of these paintings could have been purchased by his father. Yet you know I know the provenance of all these paintings. Only a handful have been owned that long."

They stopped at the vault door. He lifted her hand to his lips and kissed the back of it. Before lowering it, he asked, "Has anyone told you how beautiful your mind is?"

She laughed. "Never."

"Then they were fools who never looked past the beautiful wrapping." He saw a blush race to her cheeks.

She stared at him. "You do realize if you keep talking to me like that, I'll start believing you care for me."

"I do care for you. I've told you that. I want to take you back to the States when I leave. I want to find out where this connection goes, and I'll repeat that statement as many times as you need to hear it to believe me."

She stared at him for a long moment before opening the vault door. Then she put her hand on his arm as he opened the heavy door. "I do, too, Max. I care."

He took her hand after she locked the vault and walked to the delivery area. A warm sense of well-being boiled through him. He pulled her into him before she could turn on the lights in the delivery area. His lips found hers, and she gasped, stealing his air. She could take every molecule of oxygen from his body, and he wouldn't care. The taste of her was beyond any five-star experience he'd ever had. She formed into his body in a perfect meld of softness and curves. It was illogical and the result of a physical response to dopamine, but logic and chemicals aside, he'd never had a connection like this with any other woman. She was his. He deepened the kiss at that possessive and archaic thought. Fuck it, he didn't care. And that was yet another point that led him to believe the nexus between them couldn't be anything but serious. He never said fuck it. He never declined to investigate. When a logical reason existed, he delved deeper and verified the facts behind each decision. Yet, with this woman in his arms, he *did not care*. She was an anomaly, and for once in his life, he didn't care to dig, know why, or require an explanation. The answer to the equation did not matter, the parts were more important than the sum. Whatever it was, whatever the reason for his bliss was, he just hoped it would never fade.

He felt her push against his steel-hard cock and groaned under the contact. He pulled away from the kiss. "If you don't stop that, I may go insane."

She panted and breathlessly laughed. "You've already driven me over the edge of sanity."

"Tonight was supposed to be our night together." He dropped his forehead to hers as he spoke.

She nodded a bit. "It still can be."

"I'm not pressuring you." He pulled her in for a hug. "I won't ever do that. Take your time, and I'll respect any answer you give me. You're in control of our relationship. You're the only one who can move us to the next level."

She looked up at him. Not that he could see her in the almost complete darkness, but he could feel her movements. "Thank you."

He sighed. "You never have to thank me for being a decent human."

She laughed. "When you aren't used to dealing

with decent humans, having that privilege is worthy of gratitude. Maybe we should get the scale and find out what we're dealing with?"

He groaned and dropped his hands to her hips. "I've never been one to deviate from the job ... for any reason. You're my exception."

She reached over, and he heard her patting the wall. The lights flickered on, and she looked up at him. "I like being your exception." She glanced at the clock. "We have two hours before the delivery is due from Abrasha's residence."

"Then we should go find out what is in those frames." He grabbed the handle of the wheeled platform where she weighed the created artwork and followed her back to the vault. They weighed the frame, and he sent the pictures and dimensions to Con via his computer.

She frowned. "How can you get internet in here?" She lifted her hands and looked around her.

"I don't, but that email will be sent as soon as we leave. Economy of actions." He wouldn't tell her his ugly computer system could bore through the thickest bunker known to man. He'd developed the capability for POTUS. Guardian was also the recipient of the system due to his loyalties. The mountain they were operating under didn't have cable access;

it didn't need it. They were on solar energy provided by Doctor Jillian Marshall and an untraceable internet system that worked from under a mile of granite.

"Oh," Elena said. "Well, are you ready?"

"Let's do it." He picked up the switchblade he'd left in the storage room and depressed the indentation with the tip. The area sunk in, and the seam where the paint was slightly different popped open.

"A canvas," she whispered, and he nodded as he reached for the material. "No, don't touch it with your hands. Look how old it is. Let me get some gloves to protect the fabric from the oils on our hands."

He cocked his head to the left. Her brain was exceptional, and he loved how she was occasionally faster than he was in her area of expertise. He watched her jog out of the room before turning his attention to the canvas rolled loosely and placed in the padded compartment in the frame. If the other frames also had a painting ... why smuggle art into Russia? Unless ...

Elena came back in, handed him a set of gloves, and put her gloves on. She also placed a felt padded board on the floor. "Use this to unroll the canvas on, and please be careful." Her tone was hushed, and he could tell she wanted to be the one to unfurl the painting.

"You do it," he said, and she glanced up at him.

"Really?"

"You're trained in this."

"Okay." She licked her lips and used her fingertips to touch the very edges of the canvas. She carefully slid the painting out of the container and placed it on the felt. Carefully she loosened the roll. "Oh, God." Her hands shook. "Do you know what this is?"

"It's a Chagall." He recognized the signature on the work but not the painting itself.

"I don't recognize the painting." She leaned back and looked at him. "There were so many paintings stolen during World War II. We'll have to search the provenance of this painting."

"That's logical. If these are stolen artworks, he'd keep them here and wouldn't let you see them. You'd report them once you figured out the provenance."

"I would. Max, some paintings have been rolled in these frames for over two or three years. The damage it could be doing is insane. We have to get them all out." She stared at the other frames.

"No." He shook his head. "We have evidence of what these are, and he'll pay for these crimes, too.

We'll get them out in two weeks. Any damage that occurs in that time will be minimal, if at all, right?"

She frowned and shook her head. "Can you shut that frame?"

He inspected the mechanism and pushed the flap down. It fit seamlessly, and there was no determinable damage. "It doesn't even look like it's been opened."

She put her hand on his chest and pleaded, "We can retrieve all the paintings. I'm not an expert at restoration. These canvases must be stretched carefully and reattached to a frame in the proper humidity and under careful supervision. Max, these paintings are *history* and could have been stolen almost a hundred years ago. Those families deserve closure, they deserve to know that the paintings still exist and have a say as to what happens to them." She put her hand on his arm. "Please, can you get these out of Russia and to someone who can care for them properly? Someone who will return them to the people they were stolen from?"

In his mind, the risks of moving the paintings and drawing attention to what Guardian was doing in Russia weighed against the historical and sentimental value of the paintings. He could get them out if Guardian were willing to save them. "If we can determine they were stolen, I can contact my agency for help."

"Then let's get started." She looked at the Chagall. "I have a small area at the back of the vault where I keep a few items. We can take this canvas there and obscure it from view, just in case Abrasha makes a surprise visit."

"Then let's do it." He was ready to get to work. "What would we need?"

"A climate-controlled container. The canvases will probably return to their rolled position, especially those stored in these frames for years, so it doesn't need to be very big. We can cushion them with foam crating. I have that for shipment of Abrasha's paintings to and from his residences."

Max cocked his head. "Residences, as in plural?"

She stared at the painting in front of her but said to him, "Yes, he has several outside of Russia. I routinely refresh his collections and send out different paintings. Then, I go to the residences, change the art, ensure it is displayed correctly, and ship the replaced canvases or statues back here."

"I'll need those addresses."

She swung her gaze to him. "To get the art back after he's arrested." She nodded. "That makes sense. I have all of them on my computer."

Max smiled, not saying a word. That wasn't the only reason he needed the addresses. They had no known residences on record for Molchalin outside of Russia, and the address they had in Russia was guarded like Fort Knox. That was why they were taking him at the showing—his weakest link. The other residences could hold a treasure trove of information that could forward worldwide investigations.

"Are you ready?" She carefully picked up the felted board, giving it the excessive care the painting deserved. He stood and took the board from her until she stood, and then he gave it back to her. He followed her to a small corner with a shelving unit. He moved the items she indicated, and they set the now curling canvas on the shelf. Elena used smaller boxes lined toward the front of the shelving unit to mask the canvas. "The entire vault is environmentally controlled, so it should be fine until we can get it to a safer place."

He faced Elena and put his finger under her chin. She was glowing and radiant even with the burst blood vessels in her eyes. She loved art. It wasn't an act or a job for her. It was a conviction that flowed through her entire being. "The thought of saving these works of art is special to you, isn't it?"

She drew a deep breath and smiled at him. "This could be the reason I was put on the earth at this point in time. Saving these paintings could be the reason I *exist*."

He stared down at her. She was beautiful inside and out. "I can think of another reason you were placed here at this point in time."

She swallowed hard. "You can?"

"I can." He lowered his lips to hers and brushed them softly. "Perhaps the paintings were a secondary reason." He dipped down and kissed her again, that time parting her willing lips. The taste of her was something he'd never get enough of, and that was a fact he knew despite objective reasoning.

A jangling trill ripped through the vault. Elena jerked away from him. "The delivery is early. That's the loading dock bell." She grabbed his hand. "Come with me?"

"Always." And he meant that, too—screw objective reasoning. For the first time in his life, he would go with what his emotions told him. It wasn't liberating for him because that prickly, itchy feeling was too close to the surface. The hatred and anger for Sokolov and the mission to eliminate Abrasha were never far away. The first would be a pleasure to eliminate, and the second, a requirement. He needed to talk to the other Shadows on the case. Elena was to be protected from the situation at all costs. She couldn't see him kill either man. He had to have a future with her, and killing those two bastards could eliminate any chance he had at one with her.

CHAPTER 13

Max sat at his desk and watched Elena work. He picked up his cell phone, tapped his earpiece, and put the phone to his ear so she would think he was talking on the device and not through his comms system.

"Dude, what the hell do you need a frame for?" Con asked as a way of greeting.

"You can forget about that for the time being. The frame contained a Chagall reported as stolen during World War II. Elena found a registry of stolen artwork, and it was listed."

"So, the dude is smuggling in stolen art." That was Reaper.

"That's correct."

"How many works do you have?"

"We believe thirteen, but we haven't opened the other frames. It's a matter of preservation of the art and proper restoration to a frame. Elena doesn't have that ability, and it would take me longer than two weeks to perfect the skills to do it."

"No shit," Con said. "Try two decades."

Max rolled his eyes. Of course, the man had no idea who he was talking to. Elena glanced at him and smiled but returned to work tracking the provenance of the found canvas. He wanted to have it in case the powers that be at Guardian needed it.

"Right, anyway, contact Archangel and inform him of what we have. Getting them out of the country is the right thing to do; we should do it sooner rather than later. Elena is concerned about the deterioration of the canvases and paint due to the storage, and some of them have been here for three years."

"I can do that. Send me any information you have on the picture," Con said.

"Painting."

"Potato-Po-tot-oh." Con came back. "We can confirm Abrasha is still in China."

"Affirmative, I know," Max said. He'd checked the bastard's location before returning to the office that morning.

"How? How do you know when I only just got that confirmation about five minutes ago?"

"Con, stop being jealous." Reaper chuckled. "What about the event where we take him out?"

"We've rescheduled the showing for two weeks from now. Same location."

"I copy," Reaper said. "Same game plan?"

"Minus Merlin, and Elena is to be protected at all costs." He stared at Elena, who looked up at him. "She cannot be placed in danger."

"Noted." That was Malice. "We can exit her before the mission starts. Val, will you be able to do that?"

"And miss the fun? Guys, you're killing me here."

"I can do it," Smith said.

"No, you're the surprise element. Malice is the sniper, and Reaper is Maximus' backup. I'm the logical one to get her out." Val sighed. "I hope someone tries to stop us. I need to dismember someone."

"Why?" Smith laughed as he asked the question.

"Because someone shot you because of Molchalin." Val made that growling sound in her throat again.

"I was shot because I was a big target in a very small tunnel."

"You know what I mean," Val huffed. "I'll keep your woman safe, Maximus. You have my word on that."

"I also have four addresses for you, Con. They all belong to Molchalin." Maximus couldn't help smiling. He loved making the guy crazy.

"What? How? Where?" Con sputtered. "How are you getting this information?"

"I'll send it after the call. All are confirmed by Elena to be owned by Molchalin. She's worked on the art collections in all four locations."

"Oh." Con was silent for a moment. "You had me doubting my talents for a moment."

Max sighed. "I'm sure you're good at what you do. I'm just better." He lowered the phone while pulling out his earpiece. Both slipped into his shirt pocket.

"Why would I be in danger?" She stopped typing and turned to look at him. "You're just arresting him, right?"

"He has proven he doesn't want to be arrested, and his people have initiated gunfire on numerous occasions to give him a chance to escape. They've killed to remove him from situations where he should have been stopped." Max opened his computer and sent the addresses to Con along with the provenance that Elena had just sent to his duped email account.

"Could you be injured?" Elena asked, and he lifted his eyes from his computer screen.

"There's always that possibility, but as I said, I'm not an arresting authority."

She nodded and turned back to her computer. "How can you call on your cell phone and send emails when your jammer thing is working, and you're not connected to my internet?" She glanced over at the small box he'd placed on the desk that morning. "You said my desk phone wouldn't be affected, but I couldn't use my cell."

Max shrugged. "Different frequencies. Most cell phones operate on frequencies the government sells to wireless phone companies. The frequencies of my systems are not accessible by the government, Russian or American."

She stared at him for a moment. "Are you a spy?"

He barked out a laugh. "No, and I don't drink martinis, stirred or shaken." He assumed a British accent. "Stryker, Max Stryker."

She laughed. "When will you tell me your real name?"

"When we have taken care of Molchalin." He

couldn't compromise her or himself by divulging that information.

"Taken care … you mean arrested, right?" she asked.

"Again, I'm not an arresting authority." He shrugged. "The people who do that for the agency will have that obligation." If he didn't succeed in killing the bastard, Reaper would. He had no doubt Smith and Malice would also give their all to ensure the man didn't live. His days were numbered.

She stopped what she was doing on the computer. "It feels like you're talking around the subject."

"I am." He'd admit it. He was trying to be as transparent as he could be.

"And if I asked?"

"I'd tell you, but again, I'd ask you not to do so." He leaned forward. "One day, you'll understand everything. I will be as transparent as I can be until that time. That is as fair as I can be, given not only our lives, but the lives of my coworkers, are on the line. Should Molchalin or Sokolov find out I'm not who I say I am, or our intent be discovered before the night of the showing, I have no doubt he'd kill all of us without a second thought. Which is why I told my coworkers you were to be protected at all costs the night of the showing." If she were hurt, he'd never forgive himself.

"And before the showing?" She got up and came over to him, standing in front of him.

He took her hands and stood up, looking down at her. "Until then, I dare anyone to try to get to you. I'll tear them apart with my bare hands."

She stared up at him. "You're dangerous."

"Extremely."

"But not to me." It was a statement. Her eyes told him she knew it.

"Never." He made that vow to her, whether she understood it or not.

"Take me home, Max. Take me home and make love to me." She closed her eyes and leaned against his chest. He wrapped his arms around her and kissed the top of her head. She'd wanted him to protect her, to be her guardian against the world's evil, and he would.

CHAPTER 14

*E*lena's hands were shaking as she toweled off. Max would be waiting for her in her bedroom. She glanced at the bruises on her neck. They were ugly and glaring. She pulled the pins out of her hair and let it fall around her shoulders. Capturing it, she trailed it over her shoulders in an attempt to cover some of them. The attempt was useless and futile. The red spots in the whites of her eyes were vibrant marks, and she looked like some kind of vampire. Dark eyes surrounded by red instead of white. She pulled her wrap around her and turned off the light as she left the bathroom.

Max was in bed. His dark chest hair narrowed and trailed lower, blocked by the sheets on her bed. What was under the sheet was impossible to miss.

He reached over, flipped the sheets down on the bed's other side, and then extended his hand toward her. She drew a steadying breath and slipped off her robe.

Her insecurities grabbed ahold of her as his eyes traveled down her body. She moved her arms to cover herself, but he growled, "No. Don't do that. Don't hide from me. Come here." She reached for his hand, and he pulled her in toward him. "You're beautiful."

"I'm not." She shook her head.

"To me, you're more beautiful than the most priceless work of art. Never try to hide from me. There's no need. I see you. All of you, and I find you utterly enthralling." He lifted the sheet that covered him and draped it over her.

She reached up and touched his cheek. Her hand was shaking. God, she was so nervous. She whispered, "It's been a long time." She hadn't had sex in years. She'd tried to convince herself she was okay without the intimacy, but she wanted the relationship to work so badly that a part deep inside her wept for Max to love her. She prayed he was the man she believed him to be.

He leaned over her, his intense eyes boring into her soul. "I've never been in this position. Sex was an anatomic event before you. But tonight, we'll go somewhere special, somewhere that we can only go together." He lowered, and she thought he would kiss her, but he dropped a kiss on her cheek. He trailed kisses to her ear, then down the line of her jaw and neck.

Gasping at the sensation of his chest hair touching her breasts, she broke the trance she'd been stupefied in and reached around the man. His broad shoulders were plated with muscles. She trailed her hand down his spine as he moved over her, and she shivered when his lips found her breast. The sensations were so intense she was a little scared. She was scared of losing herself inside this mysterious man. The person who vowed to protect her and yet couldn't tell her his real name. He filled the dream of who she'd always wanted. Attractive, strong, smart, and so damn perfect he'd shattered her dream and created a reality beyond anything she could have hoped for … until Sokolov shattered everything.

He lifted his head. "What's wrong?"

She jerked. "What?"

"What did I do that you didn't like? Your body tensed and not in a good way." Max bent down and kissed her collarbone. "You can tell me if you don't like a touch or a kiss."

"No, no, you're not doing anything wrong." She wrapped her arms around his neck as he lifted. "I was thinking how perfect this was, how perfect it was until Sokolov…"

Max's eyes flashed before he shook his head back and forth slowly. "He has no place here."

She pushed his dark hair from his brow and smiled up at him. "You're right. He doesn't."

He dropped for a kiss that left her breathless. She panted as his lips moved across her skin. He moved his fingers across the skin before his lips followed. She had no idea how long he lavished her with the attention, but she was more than ready when he moved between her legs. She wrapped them around him and felt him at her sex. "Do I need a condom?"

She shook her head. "I'm on birth control." It was to regulate her periods and had nothing to do with being active sexually.

He dropped to his elbows and cupped his hands under her shoulders, pulling her down as his shaft entered her. She gasped as he entered her, and he stopped. The muscles of his neck were straining as he asked, "Did I hurt you?"

The momentary discomfort lessened almost immediately. "No. No, you didn't. Please, don't stop."

His body bowed, and he slid inside her. His size

stretched her, but the feeling of him inside her was beyond anything she could remember of the few times she'd had sex. Her body took him as he moved in and out. There was no pain, no rutting clumsiness, and no desire for the act to be over. She relished the feel of his strength over her, his hot body inside her, as the consuming sensation of being protected and cherished washed over her with ever-increasing waves of certainty.

Her body tightened, and her core ached for something … something more. "More." She whispered the word over and over. She had no idea if he knew what she needed. She only knew she didn't.

Max lifted to his knees and pulled her down the bed and up his thighs. She arched her back, and he slid inside her. "Oh, God." She wasn't sure if her words were a prayer or a plea, but the sensation was exactly what she needed. Max sped up and drove deeper. She was so close, so close. She shook her head in frustration. She needed something more. His thumb spread her sex and found her clit. He rubbed it, and Elena shattered into a billion shards of white light. He dropped on top of her, and she wrapped her arms around him as his hips moved in and out of her. When he came, she held him as tight as she could.

He moved to roll, and she tightened her hold and mumbled, "No, not yet." She needed him to be close. She needed to feel their skin melded together and to force air into her lungs as his weight was on top of her. The awareness of what had just happened sunk deep into her consciousness. Her perception pivoted; she found a new truth, and that certainty soaked so deeply inside her she knew Max had forever changed her.

When she finally loosened her grip on him, he pulled her over onto her side so they faced each other. He pushed her hair away from her face and lifted her chin with his finger. His lips found hers, and the kiss was everything she needed it to be. It was soft, a promise and a pledge. Or at least it was for her.

She lifted her leg and draped it over his legs before she wormed herself closer to him. His finger made circles and lines on her back. She shivered when she realized what he was writing. *Mine.* The possessiveness filled the tiniest of voids in her heart. There was no room for anyone but him. She was fully consumed with this man. She kissed his throat. Yes, she was his.

CHAPTER 15

Max knew when she fell asleep, but he didn't move. He wanted to hold her as much as she seemed to want to keep the connection with him. He was so far out of his depth with her. That lack of any anchor and the sensation of floating aimlessly fascinated him. Normally, research would put his world right. Questions had answers. Thoughts had logical progressions. Progressions made way for new thoughts, new processes, and new ideas. Only when it came to Elena, none of his practiced scripts would answer the questions that floated through his mind. What was love? Could a person fall in love so quickly? Were his feelings a product of the dopamine and his body's chemical reaction? And if it were a specific chemical reaction, why hadn't he felt the same when he'd had sex before? What were the variables that were different? Only his attachment to Elena. His connection.

He heard his cell phone vibrate and carefully extracted himself from Elena's hold. She woke and asked, "Where are you going?"

"My boss is calling me," he said as he got up and pulled on his boxer briefs.

"How do you know?"

"He's the only one who has the number besides you." He bent down and kissed her. "Go to sleep. I'll be back soon."

She burrowed into the pillow he was using and hummed. He grabbed his phone from his suit jacket, where it laid on a small chair. Shutting the door behind him, he glanced at the face of the phone and called back Archangel.

The CEO of Guardian growled, "Maximum."

"Force," Maximus countered.

"The painting you discovered today, do you believe it's an original?"

"I do, but what's more, Elena believes it, too. Have you read the provenance on the piece?"

"I have." There was a sigh. "Our primary focus is

Molchalin, but if we can acquire those canvases and return them to the rightful owners…"

"A good deed," Max said and sat down on the couch, looking out the window at the Black Sea. It was a beautiful area.

"More than that. Closure," Archangel said. "What do you need to get them out?"

"According to Elena, a crate that can control the humidity they're exposed to and someone who knows how to handle them on the receiving end."

Archangel was silent for a moment. "You trust her?"

"I do. She's not part of Molchalin's inner circle. He protects her because she's damn good at what she does."

"Jewell and Ethan found out how he was shielding the residences from us."

"I would expect a persona that has been stolen. Perhaps a victim of a mass tragedy such as flooding or earthquakes in a third world country."

Archangel chuckled. "Your brain is faster than any computer."

"No, not really, but I had time to consider how I'd do it while watching Elena work today."

"You care for her."

"I do. More than care for her. We have a connection." He would admit it to his boss because Jason King understood what that meant to him.

"I assumed." Jason cleared his throat. "I'll send Merlin in with the container. I'll need to know the dimensions of the largest canvas. He'll contact you when he's in country."

"Understood."

"Max?"

"Yes, sir?"

"If you have a connection with this woman, you'll want her to come home with you, right?"

"Yes, sir." There was no doubt about that.

"Someone will have to be in charge of finding the owners of these paintings and overseeing their care until that happens. I don't have a curator on the payroll, but I'd be willing to have one for this purpose. Of course, she'll have to have someone to sponsor her until the immigration paperwork is done. And she can never know you're a Shadow."

"With your permission, I will sponsor her, and this will be my last case. I find I prefer eliminating threats from behind my keyboards."

"Thank God. Yes, you have my permission and my gratitude for coming to your senses." Archangel chuckled.

"She knows I work with computers, and when

this is done, I will tell her my name as I want her to live with me."

"Jewell is running a deep background on her."

"I already have." Max rolled his eyes. As if he wouldn't have made sure he knew everything about the woman before approaching her.

"And you're a bit prejudiced, so let Jewell do it again," Archangel chided him.

"Duplication of effort, but whatever lets you sleep at night."

"Well, thank you for your permission. Now, about the other request you made."

"I want to bring that CCS operator under my wing. He has talent that hasn't been tapped based on several items I've seen. Unless he's challenged, he won't recognize what he can do."

"You'd be anonymous like you were with Jewell." That was an order, not a request.

"Yes." He didn't want the responsibility of trying to form a connection with the man. The odds of that happening were astronomical, which was why his connection with Elena was so unique.

"Then you have my approval to reach out to him. As far as we know, he's content where he is, but if you need him to relocate, we can do that, too."

"No, as long as you can provide the assets he'll

need to upgrade his systems, where he's currently located will work. I know the limitations and can design safeguards to ensure he's never located."

"When you're ready to reach out, let me know. I'll call him and let him know the contact is authorized and classified. Nothing will be said to the other node operators."

"That works."

"And Molchalin?"

"We're on a two-week timeline. The only wildcard is Sokolov. If the man approaches Elena again, I will take him out."

"Sokolov is yours when Molchalin is eliminated. The Council included him in the violet code's personnel list." Archangel continued, "But until Molchalin is gone, he's to be monitored and not eliminated."

Max didn't reply to that comment. He'd never violated a direct order, but he was damn sure going to violate that one if the bastard put a hand on Elena again.

"Did you hear me, Maximus?"

"I did."

"I'll take that as an acknowledgment of my directions." Archangel sighed. "Don't do anything that will jeopardize this assignment."

"I will kill Molchalin, then Sokolov." Max looked down the hallway at the bedroom door. "Is there anything else?"

"No. Send me the largest canvases' dimensions and pictures of how they're rolled. I'll get the case made. Merlin will contact you by the end of the week. Archangel is clear."

Max put the phone on the couch and dropped his head back. Molchalin was a cagey bastard, but he'd never expect Elena would betray him. The showing was their best chance to take the monster out. Val would keep Elena safe. Until then, he'd ask Reaper and Malice to keep an eye on Sokolov. He would be the only thing that could derail that train.

CHAPTER 16

*E*lena held the measuring tape as Max took the picture of the canvas. They left all the canvases in the frames until they had the crate to ship them out. It was a shame because she'd love to see who the paintings were by and be able to research the provenance of each one of them.

After closing the last frame, they placed it back on the easel, and she stood back and looked at the horrid painting the frame encased. Sighing, she rubbed the back of her neck. "I wish I could see them."

Max turned to her and did that little head cock to the left. "You will."

"How? We're sending them out of Russia, right?"

He nodded. "I wanted to talk to you about that.

My employer was wondering if you would oversee the restoration of the canvases and complete the provenances on each painting, determine who the owner is, if possible, and act as a curator for the paintings until they have been returned to their rightful owners or heirs."

Her hand dropped to her side, and she repeated what he'd just said in her head, trying desperately to understand how she could do that. "Where would I do this?"

"New York. Where I live." Max put his hands on her hips. "You'd work for the same people I do. On the payroll. You'd live with me."

"I'd need a work visa."

"My employer will take care of all of that."

She put her hands on his chest. "Do you mean that? Are you serious?"

"I do, and I am." He smiled. "It would mean leaving Europe. Seeing your parents would become more difficult."

"My parents." She felt a sudden shock of cold race through her. "Will they be okay? If Abrasha wants to get back at me, he could cause trouble for them."

Max shook his head. "He's not going to take any revenge. That, I promise you."

She stared at him and could read the certainty in

his eyes. "Then I say yes. My mom has friends in New York, so visiting would benefit her twofold. My dad will never set foot out of Russia. His world is the room he works in—it always has been. I'll visit as I can."

"And you'll stay with me." He pushed her for an answer.

"I will." She toed up and kissed him, and when she dropped back down, she smiled at him. "Your employer will not be sorry. I'll do an excellent job for him."

"I know you will." He took her hand, and they walked out of the vault. The sound of her phone ringing sent her jogging to her desk, and she answered in Russian, "Yes?"

"Elena, where have you been?" Abrasha snapped in response.

"In the vault, working. Is there something I can do for you, Abrasha?" She looked at Max, who visibly tensed at her words.

"The worthless paintings in the storage room will be shipping out Wednesday next week to my home in Athens."

"Wednesday? That's rushing things with the show and everything else happening."

"Do I need to hire someone else to ship them?"

"No, I can arrange for the carpenters to build the crates and coordinate with the transportation company. Do you want that empty frame, too? I could throw it in the bin."

"Do not throw anything out. That empty frame will be shipped to Athens, too. Build a crate for it the same as you would for any work of art. Protect them, Elena. They are mine, and I want them cared for as you would for a master's work."

"I can and will do that, Abrasha, but I must remind you again the reproductions are horrendous." She glanced over at Max, who crossed his arms over his chest and leaned against the desk. "Do you want me to fly to Athens and set them up in your house?"

"No, that won't be necessary. I'll probably just store them there. Hopefully, we'll use that room for the painting you're arranging the meeting for."

"It's just an introduction at this point. Max did mention the owner may be in the country at that time and would like an invitation to the showing if his and your timelines merge."

There was silence. "I will make it a point to be at the showing. I believe I may owe you a raise, Elena—very good work. I was concerned when Sokolov told me you were sleeping with this art dealer. I guess you're using your talents to my advantage."

She straightened and shook with outrage. Had she heard that right? *"What?"*

"What part of my statement didn't you understand?" The man's retort lashed her to the quick.

She ran her hand through her hair and shook her head as she blurted, "How dare you? I am your employee, not someone who would use my body to gain *you* favors. And why would Sokolov know of my relationship with Mr. Stryker? Why would either of you be concerned? I swear I have never been so insulted in my life."

"Your outrage is unnecessary, Elena. I don't care who you sleep with, but I do care that you're loyal to me and only me. Sokolov watches all of my employees. Your sudden romance was questioned; he has every right to bring it to my attention. He's an extension of me, and his loyalty is not questioned."

"But *mine* is?" She lifted her hand and slapped her leg when it dropped. "Thanks for that. Your question of my character makes all the work I've been doing for you so completely unfulfilling."

Abrasha laughed. "Deal with your emotions on your own time, Elena. Loyalty is rewarded in my world, and anyone who isn't is dealt with. Make sure you remember who you work for. Get my paintings ready to be shipped and send me the documentation when they're loaded on the truck."

"I always do," she snipped. "And for your information, I have always been loyal to you. I have always followed your instructions even when I don't understand or think you're making a mistake with your money. It isn't my place to question you. My job is to ensure you have the knowledge and connections to obtain the art you want, and I do a damn good job. Tell Sokolov to stay away from me and Max. If he confronts Max, it could cost you the *Salvator Mundi*. That is the truth. Max Stryker is *very* influential."

She glanced over at Max. His position hadn't changed, and his expression gave nothing away.

"A valid point. I will see you at the showing." The man hung up, and she slammed the phone down.

"Bastard."

Max blinked at that. "Please repeat the conversation you just had with your employer as close to verbatim as possible."

Pushing both hands through her hair, she told him exactly what the asshole had said. "I just can't believe he'd think I'd use sex to gain favors for him!"

. . .

MAX STOOD and walked over to her. "He's only showing a small portion of his colors to you. He was testing you. If you'd acted anything but outraged, he would've known you were lying."

"Sokolov knows about us and told Abrasha. What has he seen? What does he know about us? I just can't." She covered her face with her hands, and Max's arms enveloped her.

"Sokolov has made a logical conclusion. I don't leave your home at night and have checked out of my hotel. If he hadn't told Abrasha, he'd be stupid. And now, we have his word he'll be at the showing."

"Can we get the canvases secured in the case and out of here by Wednesday?" She lifted her head off his chest. "Sokolov is watching. God, why didn't that register? He had a picture of you at the front door of the office. Do you think he has cameras in my apartment? Dear God." She covered her face with both hands. Had he been watching her? She felt so violated.

He grabbed her hands and pulled them away from her face. "No, he has no camera in your home."

"How do you know that?"

"Because I checked. There are no monitors of any kind except for your internet access. They know what sites you go to and what you do when you're online." Max lowered so he was looking directly into her eyes. "I would never let anyone watch us. What happens between us is private; no one but us will ever know what happens in your home. Do you understand?"

She nodded. "You're sure?"

"Absolutely positive." When he smiled, all the shame she'd felt evaporated.

"Okay." She nodded. "Okay. So, we need to move the canvases before Wednesday. How do we get the case in and out without Sokolov knowing?"

Max smiled at her and winked. "Leave that to a magician I know."

She narrowed her eyes. "You're talking around things again."

He nodded. "I am."

"And I shouldn't ask questions."

"Nope," he said as a smile spread across his face.

"I'm getting good at that."

"Very good." He laughed.

"Fine. Keep your secrets." She rolled her eyes. "I need to make calls to carpenters and the trucking company."

He tapped her on the butt when she turned around. "Fresh," she said over her shoulder.

"Absolutely," he agreed and went to his desk to do

something on the ancient-looking computer that could do things she didn't understand. Maybe it was better she didn't.

When she finished arranging the carpenters and the shipment of the artwork, it was way past time for dinner. They closed up, she activated the alarms, and they walked hand in hand down the boardwalk to her regular café.

After they were seated at her regular table, they ordered tea and their meal. The sound of diners' conversations was quiet in the background as most people had already had their dinner and left to go to the evening's activities or home.

Elena laughed at Max's antidotes about his sister's attempts to fix him up and the types of women she'd thought Max would go for. "She was a model and didn't eat. Literally, she drank all her calories, and any energy she got was because she snorted it up her nose." Max groaned. "My mother drew the line after that and then proceeded to grill Martha on how she knew a person who used cocaine as an energy source."

"That's a good question. How did she?" Elena asked as she sipped her after dinner tea.

"Martha's a photographer, and they'd met during a shoot. Martha had no idea the woman was as dependent on chemicals as she was. Or so she said. I think she was desperate for me to have a girlfriend."

"She worries about you, true?" Elena asked as he took a sip of his tea.

"Worries about me?" His brow furrowed. "That could be the case, but I think she wants me to be normal, and working with my computer systems in my basement isn't, at least in her opinion. She once told me serial killers were spawned in that fashion."

Elena barked out a laugh. "She did not say that!"

"She absolutely did, and it was at dinner with my entire family around the table." Max laughed. "It's a good thing she's the baby of the family because I'm sure if my brothers had said that my mother would have ended them."

"She sounds like a character."

"She'll love you," Max said. "All my family will."

She wasn't so sure. She hoped that was the case, but in reality, what would cause them to love her? She was a stranger. "How could you possibly know that?"

"They'll love you because I do." He stared at her and reached for her hand. She blinked at him, and her mouth slackened.

"What did you say?"

He smiled at her and whispered so only she could

hear him, "I'm a man of logical enterprises, yet there's nothing logical about the feelings I have for you. They won't change any of the facts, but they do change me. You have changed me. I'm falling in love with you, Elena. Please tell me you feel the same way."

She snapped her mouth shut and nodded. "I do. God, I do. If I admitted it, I thought you'd run away as fast as possible."

"I'm never going to run away from you. Only toward you." He lifted her hand and kissed the back of it. She shivered, and her core clenched at the sexy and gentle gesture.

"You should take me home now, Max." Her whisper was just as quiet but edged with desperation.

He stood and dropped a roll of notes on the table, not bothering to count them for the bill. He extended his hand to her, and they moved through the small establishment and out the door. She wrapped her hand around his bicep and stared up at him. "How am I so lucky?"

He covered her hand with his and smiled down at her. "Luck has nothing to do with what we have. I have to believe it's destiny. I'm not a firm believer in fate, luck, or destiny, but there's no logical divination as to why we found each other, how circumstances led me to this assignment, or …"

"Or?" She smiled and looked up at him. His face had turned to stone. "What is it?"

"Don't look back, but we're being followed." He tightened his grip on her hand when she jumped.

A jolt of fear shot through her. "Are you sure?"

"Positive. One man on our left back about fifty feet. I'm going to stop and kiss you. I want you to look discretely and see if you recognize him."

"I can do that." She nodded and he stopped, turned to her, and tipped her head in exactly the angle she needed to see the man following her. Max moved a bit and blocked her view.

He whispered against her lips. "Sokolov?"

"Yes," she responded. Max kissed her and then started them on the way back to her apartment. "Why's he doing this?"

"He's a loose cannon. I don't think he likes the fact Abrasha listens to you." Max patted her hand.

"What do you mean?"

"You told Abrasha that approaching me could lose him the opportunity for the painting."

"I did," she agreed.

"What's the one thing Abrasha cares for more than anything else?"

"Money," she answered. There was no doubt about that now.

Max chuckled. "If you hadn't found out about him, what would your answer have been?"

"Art. Specifically, paintings, and he's obsessed with the *Salvator Mundi*."

"So, it stands to reason he'd warn Sokolov off any approach. This is his way of defying Abrasha." Max paused on the boardwalk, and they stared out at the Black Sea as waves gently lapped the shore. There was barely a whisper of air moving, and it was heavy with the scent of blossoms from the gardens scattered along the pathway. The moon, now waning, reflected its yellow-gold light across the water and painted a magical scene.

"He terrifies me." She shivered and laid her head against his arm as she looked out, not seeing the beauty but rather feeling the threat the man behind them constituted.

Max put his arm around her and pulled her tight against him. "He will never touch you again." His voice, while low, held a threat.

She looked up at him. "Max?"

"Yes?"

"How dangerous are you?"

"There are very few who are more dangerous than I," he replied as he stared out at the sea.

She dropped her head against him again. "Deadly?" She wasn't sure if she wanted the answer, but something told her Max wasn't an arresting entity because arresting Abrasha wasn't on the table. The thought had been there for some time, and she wasn't afraid of the concept. The information she'd read about Abrasha ... he was a monster.

He turned to stare at her. "Very."

The golden hue of the moon illuminated one side of his face, leaving the other in darkness. She should be terrified of the ability he held, but that was only a part of him like the shadow on his face. He was a mix of light and dark, and his light outshone the dark when he was with her. He was two people in one. His single word cut through the darkness. It stilled her thoughts and merged them into a crystal-clear realization. Maybe he wasn't a spy, but he was there to kill Abrasha. His team was there to ensure it happened. They started to walk again toward her apartment, and she found she was comforted by his words and confidence. He was her shield against the coming storm. "Is it wrong to say I'm glad you are? That you're protecting me?"

He dropped his arm over her shoulder, tucked

her close, and whispered, "It isn't wrong." They walked farther before he said, "You've figured out what's happening."

"I believe I have." She nodded. "I'm sure there's a reason it's happening this way."

"You've seen a few of the reasons," he agreed.

She had. The atrocities were beyond her wildest imagination. "Sokolov?"

He looked down at her and lifted his eyebrow. "What do you think?"

She stopped and stared up at him. "Not because of me."

Max shook his head. "For his crimes against humanity. As reparation for those who couldn't protect themselves and were victimized, tortured, and murdered by the monsters both men are."

She stared at him. "How do you not get lost in all the darkness?"

He smiled. "We are the darkness. We live in the light only because of the people we love. *Love* is the beacon that brings us home. Darkness's destiny has always been bound and controlled by the light."

She toed up, kissed him, and realized he was, in fact, her destiny. She was his, but in so many ways, he was hers. They completed each other. She would be his light, and together, they were whole.

CHAPTER 17

Max turned off the lights in the apartment after scanning it again to make sure there were no new listening devices or cameras. His cameras were still up, and he reviewed the film from the day in fast forward while Elena closed up the office. But he wasn't one to take chances. Checking was second nature. He made his way to the bedroom, where Elena was lying under the sheet. The small lamp on the bedside cast a mellow light over her body. Her curves draped with the linen were a siren's song.

He dispatched his clothes as he stared at her. Her eyes were hungry, and damned if she wasn't licking her lips as he stripped. As she sat up and the draped sheet fell away, he drank in the beauty of the woman before him. Elena crawled to the end of the bed and sat on her heels. She reached for his cock, and the feel of her hand on his shaft spun his eyes backward in his head. He ran his hands through her thick hair and held on when he felt her soft tongue trace the cap of his shaft. His hand tightened when she took him into her mouth. He could tell she hadn't done that act before. She was hesitant, and he carefully encouraged her but didn't force her. Her sweet submission heightened the sensations. Fuck, he could lose himself in her. In fact, he had. He'd lost himself to her.

When she choked, he withdrew and dropped to his knees in front of her. "I'm sorry," she said, wiping her mouth. "I wanted to do that right."

"You were perfect. Absolutely perfect. Now, it's my turn." He lowered her to the bed and draped her legs over his shoulders, pulling her to the edge of the bed. He kissed her lower stomach and then trailed lower. Gooseflesh rose against his tongue as he kissed her thigh. He separated her sex with his fingers and blew softly against her heated flesh before lowering to taste her.

Perfection.

His mind clicked off the reasons she tasted so good to him. The biology of sex was something he knew. However, none of that mattered. He didn't care what chemical reaction was driving his desire because he *did not care*. At that moment, with this woman, there was nothing else. His mind quieted, his world focused to a pinpoint, and he relaxed into the peace she gave him.

She arched under him, and he belted her waist to the bed with his arm as he ramped up his feasting. He entered her with one finger and curled it, rubbing a bit as he sucked her clit into his mouth. She came undone and grabbed his hair with her hands. Her shocked gasp when she shattered was beautiful music. He licked her a couple more times before he rose, put one knee on the bed, and lifted her legs. He drove down into her, deeper and faster, the way she'd needed the night before. He lost himself in the sensations, and when her body grabbed at him and she tightened, he let go, exploding inside her.

He froze above her and stared at the beautiful picture below him. Her dark brown hair spread across the bed, and her body flushed with a crimson hue of satisfaction. She opened her eyes and smiled at him. He dropped for a kiss, nearly folding her in half, but both adapted as they shared each other's taste. Then he lifted away and helped her to the top of the bed, where he folded her into him and held her until she fell asleep. When he moved away from her, she simply sighed and grabbed his pillow. He put on his boxer briefs and grabbed his comm device.

That fucker Sokolov was stalking *her*, not him.

"Sokolov followed us from the office."

Con snorted. "Bastard."

"You don't know the half of it," Reaper said. "He's watching the apartment building now. Fucker is jacking off."

"I'm sure you're aware he's acting like a sexual predator," Smith added.

"Escalation is almost guaranteed." That was Val. "He got a sexual thrill out of beating her. He wants to do it again."

Max was aware of all of that. He'd come to that conclusion as soon as he saw the bastard following them.

"Which is why he's spanking his wanker in the bushes," Malice chimed in.

"Gross, dude," Val said.

"What? Would you prefer the five-knuckle shuffle? Spanking his monkey? Corralling tadpoles? Milking the lizard." Malice laughed when Val growled.

"If we can get back to business?" Max dropped his head into his hand and yawned. He wanted to go back to bed with his woman.

"Sure, what business did you want to discuss besides Sokolov waxing the dolphin?" Con added with a laugh.

"All of you are disgusting," Val said, and Max could almost hear her eye roll.

"I didn't say anything," Smith objected.

"Nor did I," Reaper added.

"Ditto," Max said. He was trying to get Merlin information.

"Fine, Mal and Con, you are disgusting."

"Thank you," they said at the same time.

"Anyway," Max sighed. "Sokolov is watching Elena, which means he could be watching the office during the day. If he's fixated on her, it's a certainty Merlin will have to go into the building, deliver the crate, load the canvases, and get out without showing the alarm as being deactivated, and he'll have to do it at night when we're not there."

He could hear Con typing. "That's his favorite time of day. Do we have the specs on the system?"

"I dropped it in your box this afternoon," Max said, yawning again.

"You did? I didn't get a notification." Con's

fingers were flying across the keyboard. "Wait, how did you do that?"

"Do what?" Max drawled.

Con made a weird sound and asked, "How did you disable my notifications?"

"I have no idea what you're talking about." He smiled despite being tired.

Reaper laughed. "Someone who only works at it part-time is better than you, Con."

"No, no, this is not okay," Con said, and Max swore the guy's fingers would punch a hole through the keyboard. "Nobody can do that. You can't. Not unless…"

Max chuckled. "Get the information to Merlin. He has to be in and out by Tuesday morning. The art is being packed then."

"Wait, I want to know what unless means," Smith interjected.

"Ah, nothing. Nothing. It can't be that. I'll figure it out," Con answered, distracted by whatever he was doing.

"Sure. I have no doubt." Max chuckled.

"Hey, this is payback for the way you pester Fury. Damn, what goes around comes around, Con." Reaper laughed.

Con groaned, "No, no, this is bullshit. This isn't possible. I have to get ahold of Jewell."

Max laughed. "If it isn't possible, how did it happen, Con? Maximus is clear." He took out his earbud. He'd watched Con torment Fury for long enough. It was time for him to get a taste of his own.

He got up and returned to the bedroom, sliding between the sheets and pulling Elena back into him. She made a sound he swore was a purr and snuggled against him. He closed his eyes and pictured Sokolov in his mind. The target on the man had just come into focus. They had less than a week before the showing. Less than a week before he and that bastard would finally meet.

CHAPTER 18

Merlin walked down the vault hall and gazed at the works of art secured behind the system he'd just circumvented. In his hand was an oversized briefcase made to hold the canvases hidden in the frames in the storage room.

He'd received all the information Maximus had sent him and the tidbits Con had given him. Maximus somehow had his cell phone number. Only two other people in the world had that number. He didn't ask the Shadow how he'd gotten it. Respect. Merlin chuckled when he opened the storage room door. A sticky note was on the first frame. "Push indention on back of frames. Wear these gloves."

"Well, that makes it boring." He put the case down and opened it. There were thirteen slots for the rolled canvases. He changed his gloves from the anti-static ones he wore to those left for him.

He could have rushed the job, but there was no hurry. The security system to get into the vault was complex, true. Still, it was easily defeated, especially because the camera system and bugging devices were defeated outside and inside the office.

The compartments hidden in the frames were brilliant. He'd put that idea in his bag of tricks. One by one, he carefully moved the rolled canvases to the specific slot made for them in his case. The case would hold a change of clothes and other items, hiding the four-inch interior that ran the length of the case and shielding the canvases from airport security and environmental concerns.

If the paintings were, in fact, stolen, he was happy to steal them back. He was a thief with a conscience—a modern-day Robin Hood. He chuckled as he closed a frame and replaced it on the easel, moving to the next. He wouldn't be caught dead in tights and those damn pointy shoes, but he was damn good at giving back to those who'd been screwed.

His phone vibrated, and he frowned, stopping what he was doing to look at the damn thing. He sat beside his case and answered, "Maximus, these frames are ingenious."

"They are. Any problems?"

He let out a snort in response. "As if."

"How did you dupe the fingerprint?"

"You and your lady had dinner tonight. When you left, the water glass may have disappeared off the table. She's beautiful, by the way." There was silence at the end of the line. "You didn't see me, did you? You were a bit occupied."

"Medium height, I'd say five feet ten or eleven inches tall, dark hair, glasses, wearing a blue henley with a sweater, black slacks, Hermes belt, and I believe your shoes were handmade. Italian."

"You're good. Not Italian. I had them made in London."

"By an Italian artisan," Maximus replied.

Merlin chuckled. "Possibly. I didn't inquire. To what do I owe this lovely chat? Would you like a referral to my shoemaker?"

"Thank you, no. I'm more of a tennis shoe and t-shirt person."

Merlin laughed. "Not tonight. That was a Tom Ford suit, or I'm purple with pink dots."

Maximus laughed. "It was. Will you need

anything special at the airports to get that case through security?"

"No, we've shielded it. Why? Do you have a magic wand?"

"More like a magic keyboard. The Russian equivalent of the TSA doesn't have redundancy or firewall protections, so manipulating it is child's play."

"Ah, so you're a computer whiz, too?"

"I dabble."

"Is that how you got my number? The two people who have it wouldn't give it out."

Maximus chuckled. "Possibly. You have my number if you need assistance."

"Why wouldn't I call Con, Jewell, or Brando?" They were his normal points of contact for assistance.

"I'm faster and in your time zone." That statement was not bravado, which reinforced his belief the man was more than a computer whiz—he was dangerously good. No one should have been able to get his number. It didn't exist, according to Archangel.

"Appreciate the offer, but I'm good." Merlin glanced at the frame on the floor. "You said there was a canvas that needed to lay flat?"

"The canvas rolled back on itself, so instead of

damaging it, we put it back in the frame. The one to your right. You shouldn't be sitting down on the job, by the way."

Merlin jerked and searched the room. "Well, hello, Maximus." He stood and walked over to the small camera in the corner of the room. "Are you going to tell me how you're getting a signal out or how we're talking when this vault should shield everything?"

There was a chuckle on the other end. "And this is why you should call me when you need assistance."

Merlin nodded. "Does Archangel know you're offering your services?"

"He will. Call if you're backed into a corner."

"I will. Thanks."

"You take care of those paintings, or Elena will have both our heads on a platter."

Merlin laughed. "I'd like to meet her someday."

"Hands off, my newly minted friend." The connection ended with that comment.

Merlin barked a laugh and got to work after taking the camera down and putting it in his pocket. He'd take it apart later and figure out what Maximus knew that he didn't. Electronics fascinated him.

CHAPTER 19

*E*lena sat in the grass while Max bought them sweets and tea from a vendor about ten feet away. They'd spent the morning at the Sochi Arboretum. The expansive gardens were beautiful and hosted a variety of plants from all over the world. The scents were amazing, and the colors were things she'd hold in her mind's eye as she tried to paint the memories. They'd taken the cable car to the top of the hill and had a picnic lunch while they enjoyed the unending view of the mountains, the sea, and the city of Sochi.

Max in a suit was something to behold, but Max wearing jeans and a henley was just about the sexiest thing in the world. The fabric pulled across his wide shoulders and outlined the powerful form that the suit had hidden. She accepted the paper cup holding her tea and a napkin with a fancy chocolate with a creamy pistachio filling.

She sighed and closed her eyes.

"Happy?"

She finished the candy and nodded. "Yes, this has been the best day. I've lived here for almost four years and never went to the arboretum or up to the top of the hill on the cable car."

"I know what you mean. There are plenty of sights and places I haven't experienced in New York. It seems like life can consume all your time, and people forget to pause and see what wonderful things are before them."

She nodded in agreement and took a sip of her tea. "He'll be back soon."

"Abrasha?"

"Yes." She glanced over at Max. "What do I need to do?"

"What do you normally do for a showing?"

She drew a breath and said, "We must go to Krasnaya Polyana tomorrow. I'll inspect the rooms we will use and talk with the manager about additional security that Abrasha requires. My carpentry team will set up the backings, and electricians will run the lighting the next day. The art is exclusively from

Abrasha's Sochi compound. The paintings will arrive the day before the showing. We'll stay there and ensure the placement is perfect. The lodge is responsible for security, although Sokolov and his people will be there whenever Abrasha arrives and during the transportation of the art."

"Do you need to crate it before it is shipped?"

"No, that was done before I met you. Sokolov or his people will direct the transportation company to the crates, and they will follow the truck there."

"And the night of the event?"

She laughed. "I stress. There always seems to be something that goes wrong. The caterer doesn't have the right champagne, a string of lights goes dark, or Abrasha demands another painting shown at the last moment." She shrugged. "But this time, I will be scared."

"You will never be in danger."

"I know. But what if I lose sight of the woman …"

"Val."

She nodded. Val. Why couldn't she remember the woman's name? Lord. She was a nervous wreck already.

"It will be her job to keep close to you. Do what you normally do, but when she indicates it's time to leave, do it. Make whatever excuses you need to make, but go."

"Okay." She glanced at him. "You'll be okay?"

He smiled and winked at her. "You bet."

"You're so confident." She dropped her head to his shoulder and enjoyed the warmth of the sun on her shoulders.

"Training," he said, and she made a humming sound. That was why she was confident in her work. She was constantly learning. There was always some knowledge to glean from the past or current work in the field.

Her cell phone chimed, and she frowned and pulled it out of her purse. "Abrasha." She answered it. "Yes?"

"I've changed the date of the shipment to Greece to tomorrow."

"Tomorrow." She glanced at Max. "The company came to pick them up the day before yesterday as was your directive."

There was a long silence, and then he swore. "Can you get them back?"

"I could try. Is there a problem?"

"Someone wanted to inspect one of the paintings," Abrasha mumbled something under his breath.

"When?"

"During the showing."

"Even if I called them back now, they might not be back in time for that."

Abrasha let out a low string of horrible words before he hung up.

She blinked and repeated the conversation to Max. "I'm not sure if I'm to turn them back or not?"

"Let's go to the office."

She sighed and accepted his hand. "See what I mean about last minute things going wrong?"

He chuckled and offered her his arm. "This isn't a concern. By the time the paintings return or arrive in Greece, Abrasha won't be worried about them."

She glanced up at him. "No, he won't, will he?" A lightness lifted her a bit, and she immediately felt horrid because she knew Abrasha wouldn't live past the night of the showing, which was a heavy burden. She should be appalled by the thought. She should want to warn him and stop the violent swipe of justice from being dealt, but after reading the proof of his horrendous deeds, seeing the photos, and getting to know Max, she didn't feel the need to warn the murderer. Did that make her a horrible person? Did it diminish her morality? Perhaps. But it was something she could live with.

"What are you thinking?" Max asked her as they walked.

"Hmm?" She glanced up at him. "Oh, I'm rationalizing my morality."

He chuckled. "So, light thoughts, huh?"

She laughed softly. "I just can't feel regret for being part of what you're going to do. I wondered if that meant I was morally corrupt."

"And what did you decide?" Max looked both ways before they crossed the street, heading back to her office.

"That he shouldn't have done the crimes. He made the choices to do the atrocities he's done. He should be held accountable for them." Or, in that case, die because of them.

Max covered her hand that was tucked through his elbow. "He's following us again."

She sighed and shook her head. "Why?"

"We believe he's fixated on you. When he roughed you up, it gave him some sense of exhilaration."

She looked up at him and stumbled a bit. He caught her and put his arm around her. "You think he wants to hurt me again?"

"I do. But he won't ever have the opportunity." Max glanced down at her. "We're almost at the end."

"I know." She paused, then asked, "You're sure the canvases were taken out of the vault?" She couldn't believe someone could bypass the alarms, remove the canvases, put them in a case, and take them out of one of the most secure places in Russia without anyone knowing.

"I'm positive. We should know tomorrow that they're safe and who the artists are."

"The fact that someone wants to see the paintings, do you think he's already sold one of the canvases?"

"Probably. We'll keep an eye out at the showing to ensure no one else from our watch list is involved."

"Watch list." She shook her head. "There are so many horrible people you have a list?"

"The world is full of people who seek power at any cost. My organization ensures those without voices, power, or means are protected and represented."

She could imagine him at the forefront of that war. He was driven and so smart, and he was hers. That knowledge filled her with a peace she hadn't felt before. "And you can do this from behind a computer?"

"I'm very good at what I do." He chuckled. "Far better at that portion of the job than this."

She glanced up at him. "And yet you said there were very few better than you at this portion of your job."

"Correct," he acknowledged.

"What do you think the odds of us meeting in any other way would be?"

"Would you like to do the math, or were you speaking hypothetically?" Max chuckled when she made a face at him.

"Don't expect me to do the math. Two plus two has always equaled five in my book." She faked a shiver. "I hate math."

Max stopped at the office door, and she entered her code while he turned his back, ensuring Sokolov saw he was intentionally not looking, she supposed. After she opened the door and they entered the office, she felt Max's hand on her shoulder, stopping her before she opened the interior door. "Someone's been here. Don't say anything until I clear the room."

She nodded and opened the door. How did he know someone had been in the office? She frowned at him but went to her desk and picked up the phone to call the transport company. She pulled her drawer out and looked for her phone book—a small black ledger in which she'd put her contact numbers. Closing the drawer, she opened the one on the right. There it was. She held it up and stared at it. "How did you get in the wrong drawer?"

Max glanced over at her and nodded. He got the message. Someone had gone through her desk. After dialing the number of the contracted trucking company, she asked if they had a location on the truck. She was put on hold and watched as Max walked around the office, appearing to look at his phone as he wandered. He stopped by her desk and sat down. She smiled at him, and he winked at her, tapping the desk. She got it. There was a bug in her desk. When the trucking company came back online, she requested the direct and expedited return of the cargo. She powered up her computer and typed an email to Abrasha indicating she'd done as he'd asked while they chatted about their day. Max suggested dinner, and she agreed immediately. "I'm done here."

She put the phone book into the correct drawer, turned off her computer, and they exited the office with little fanfare. As they walked down the sidewalk, she asked, "How many devices?"

"One. But as we aren't returning to the office again, it's of zero consequence." He shrugged and held her hand as they walked across the street.

"How did you know someone had gone into the office?"

"Old school tech." He chuckled. "I put a small thread in the joint of the door when we left. The thread was missing, so someone had entered and exited the office area."

"It had to be Sokolov." She shivered, and he tightened his grip on her hand. He'd noticed her reaction, and that warmed her in a way nothing else could. Max noticed everything about her, and that made the moment bearable. He was with her so she could examine Sokolov's motives without feeling out of control. "I can't … He's crazy, isn't he? Why would he want to hear what I say?"

"He's always heard what you said. Remember the jamming device I put into the office?"

She blinked and stopped walking. "I thought that was a precaution."

"No, that was a fix. I took it with us every night. I'm surprised it took him this long to plant another bug."

"What about my apartment?"

"We'll check it when we get there. Anything he can put in the apartment, I can circumvent." Max squeezed her hand reassuringly. "Tomorrow, we'll be in the mountains, and he won't be there until Abrasha arrives."

She nodded and smiled as Max bent down to kiss her. "Thank you."

"For what?" he asked as he lifted away from her.

"For being here, for having a connection with me. For …"

"Loving you?" he asked, cocking his head to the left.

"It seems strange to say it, especially because we so recently met. Are we being foolish?" It hadn't been all that long ago, yet it seemed she'd known him her entire life. She stepped closer to him. "But it doesn't feel that way, and I don't think time could change what I feel."

"Or what I feel." He smiled down at her. "Let's get something to eat and then go home to pack for the event."

She nodded and walked with him to their café. It was time to prepare for the show and the rest of her life.

CHAPTER 20

The road through the Caucasus Mountains meandered and at any other time would have been enjoyable. That day, it was a prep for the mission. Before leaving, he'd double-checked the car he'd rented through a service to ensure they could talk freely.

"So, we need an extra room off the venue?"

"Yes, for a meeting between Abrasha and the prince who supposedly owns the *Salvator Mundi*."

"And that would be where ..." Her voice trailed off.

"No, it'll provide access to him, but it won't be there." He glanced over at her. "You won't be involved with it. You'll be gone before I approach him to meet the prince."

She nodded, and he reached over and covered her hand with his. "I need to know you'll be able to do this."

She nodded. "All I have to do is my job. You'll do the rest."

"And follow Val's directions."

"Immediately," she added. "I know this is the right thing to do. I just feel ... guilty for setting him up."

"You aren't doing that. I am." Max made that point again. "None of this is on you. You're doing your job. I'm doing mine, and Abrasha will pay for the crimes he's committed."

She squeezed his hand. "I know that rationally, but still, he's going to be killed." She shook her head. "Knowing that is hard."

"It is." It was something she would have to internalize and come to terms with. Unfortunately, he couldn't help her.

"The turnoff is just up here," Elena said as they approached the lodge. The area was in the middle of a dense forest, and they'd passed several rivers that wound through the mountains. He pulled up to the front and parked the car. A man greeted Elena as they entered.

"Elena, there you are. We're ready for you. The

carpenters and electricians have already been here to check the rooms."

"Thank you, Anatoly." She turned to him and continued in Russian. "This is Max; he's working with me for this showing. We'll need an additional room tonight for a meeting between important guests and my employer."

"Of course, of course. I have several near the exhibition hall. If you'll come with me, we can do the inspection of the venue and select the room you'll need. Of course, there'll be an added charge for the facility."

"Of course," Elena agreed. Max trailed behind the two as they reviewed the show's details and discussed catering, alcohol service, and security. He paced off the dimensions of the hall and observed all the exits, windows, and where the staff would enter and exit. As they discussed security, he listened and noted where the staff security would be posted. Depending on how many men came with Abrasha, exiting the venue with Abrasha could get dicey. He didn't care if Abrasha was alive or dead when he took him out of the lodge. Either way, the message he would send would be a gruesome and obvious message not only to Molchalin's allies but to everyone who thought they were above the law.

After about an hour's discussion with Anatoly, Elena returned alone to speak with him. "I need to talk to the electrician and the carpenter next. Do you need anything before I do that?"

"No. I'm fine; the room you selected for the meeting will work. I'm going to take a walk outside. Sokolov isn't here. I've confirmed he's still in Sochi. You're safe."

She smiled at him. "Thank you. I'll meet you in the room?" She handed him an old-fashioned key with a room number on it. "I shouldn't be too long, then we can go to dinner. They have a lovely café with outdoor seating. The stars are beyond beautiful."

He leaned down and kissed her. "They couldn't compare to you."

She smiled up at him. "Don't get lost in the woods."

"Never."

A person called her name from the other end of the hall, and he kissed her again before she spun around and approached the man who'd called her. They embraced like old friends and started talking. Max ducked out of one of the exits and headed to his meeting.

The forest cloaked their meeting. Reaper, Malice,

Smith, and Val emerged from beside the trail as he approached the small clearing near the waterfall.

Maximus unfolded the schematic of the building he'd taken from the Sochi public works archives.

"There have been modifications to the room since the blueprints I sent you were published. Here and here are doors leading back into the lobby of the resort. There are no exits in this hallway. In this hallway, there's an exit next to the breakout room we've chosen for the prince to meet Abrasha." Maximus looked up at Smith. "How are preparations coming?"

Val chuckled. "We have it. I had to call Harbinger for a little advice, but we've perfected it."

Smith grunted. "Just what I've always wanted to do. Not." He crossed his arms over his chest, and Val leaned against him. "Oh, poor Smith. You'll survive." She looked over at Reaper. "Won't he?" That was a direct challenge. Maximus cocked his head to the left and glanced at Reaper.

"He will." Reaper nodded. "Malice will support Maximus on the exit plan, and then he'll have our back as shit hits the fan."

"I've got it. We've got everything prepped," Malice said. "My long-range rifle is secured and hidden. I know the route and have run it during the day and several times in the dark. I'll walk it again before security shows up to make sure there are no impediments to my sprint."

Maximus nodded. "Good. I'll set up the first round of diversions. Are you good with setting the second?" He looked at Reaper.

"Yep. I have it. Mal will go with me to set them up. We're good."

"Invitations?" Val asked.

Max reached into his inside suit pocket and extracted two invitations, handing one to Val and Reaper. "Yours, Val. Reaper, this is yours. Smith, you must be here no later than twenty-one hundred hours." He pointed to the exact spot on the map.

Smith nodded. "I'll be there."

"I'll let you know what the dress code is," Val said, smiling. "For the first time, he's got more clothes in our luggage than I do."

Reaper chuckled at Smith's pained expression. "Taking one for the team, Smith. We appreciate it."

"If it is the way we get rid of him, I'll take two." Smith's expression told everyone he wanted Molchalin removed as much as they did.

"What about Sokolov?" Val asked.

"He's mine." Maximus looked at each of the Shadows one at a time. "Mine."

"Understood." Malice nodded his head. "We've all

been there, not the same circumstances, but we know what it's like to ensure those we love don't have to worry about the past haunting them."

"Then we're set."

"Not quite," Malice said. "Con told us you couldn't drop that information in the system without them knowing. Jewell confirmed it, and both of them are in a tizzy about you circumventing their safeguards. How did you do it?"

Maximus smiled. "If I told you, I'd have to kill you."

Reaper's eyebrow rose. "I could push the issue."

"Why?" Val said. "He's good. He's on our side, right? The bosses don't have an issue with it, or we'd have orders to determine how he did it. We don't. All we have is Con whining. Jewell hasn't said squat to us. And watching Con get some of his own is funny as hell. It's about time."

All four of them laughed, and Smith pointed to his ear. Maximus smiled. He knew Con had heard the entire meeting and was fine with that. He glanced at his watch. "We have twenty-seven hours until the show. Last call for alibis."

He looked at the other assassins. "We're good, and Con said to tell you Abrasha has landed in Sochi," Val said.

"I know." Malice smiled. "He's en route to his compound, where he'll spend the night before coming up here tomorrow night. He never spends the night outside of his compound when he's here."

"Are you ready to go?" He looked at Malice.

"Good to go," Malice said.

"I'm ready, too," Reaper agreed. "As long as you're wearing your comms tomorrow night."

"I will be." Max turned around and walked back down the path he'd traveled. The die had been cast, and the following night, Abrasha Molchalin would pay for the damage he'd done to the innocents of the world.

CHAPTER 21

"You look stunning." Max walked a circle around Elena, who wore a sleeveless black gown that had a slit up her thigh. A bit high for her liking, but it was the style. The material clung to her curves, and she hoped she didn't look lumpy. A small gold chain glistened around her neck, a graduation gift from her mother, and she had matching drop earrings her father had purchased. Max had warned her she wouldn't be coming back for anything, so she wore what was most important to her. Her hair was swept up in a smooth coil, with curls strategically escaping and framing her face.

"Thank you." She waved at her face. "I usually

don't worry about makeup, but tonight, I needed something to hide behind. Does that make sense?"

He smiled and touched her chin with his finger, tilting her face up. "You're absolutely beautiful without makeup, but I understand the need for a little armor tonight."

She took a deep breath and blew it out slowly. "I'm worried I'll screw up."

"You won't. Just do what you normally do."

"And listen to Val."

"At all costs."

"He should be here soon." She glanced at the clock. "And we should go downstairs. Guests will start arriving shortly." She brushed his tux's collar. "You look amazing."

He smiled at her. "You've got this."

"I know." She nodded.

They made their way to the event. The facility security nodded as they passed. She and Max had been in and out of the venue all day and were known to everyone. She went directly to the small room in the back where the champagne and small bites would be loaded onto trays and circulated through the crowd. "Is the champagne properly chilled?"

"Yes, ma'am, and the servers are on a timed release as per our conversation. Champagne service for the first half hour, then food trays are mixed in," the kitchen lead said. She looked around. "We have more than enough for the number of people attending tonight."

"Good. Thank you. If you have any problems, don't hesitate to come get me."

"I will, but we're fine," the woman assured her.

She smiled and returned to the venue. The lights were now dimmed, and the spotlights on the paintings were in full view. She moved to the Monet and adjusted the light to the left to draw on the lighting over the pond. Each painting was mounted and highlighted perfectly, but she had to check one last time. By the time she'd finished, guests were arriving. The manager of the resort was taking invitations and checking the people off as they came in. Max lingered in front of the Chagall, and she walked up to him. "I have to go play hostess."

He smiled at her. "I'll join you." He extended his arm, and she slid her hand into the crook of his arm. "Breathe."

"I am." Wasn't she?

As they reached the front of the venue, habit clicked into place, and she greeted each of the couples as they walked through the door. She asked about children, pets, and vacations. She didn't know the people but remembered what she'd learned from the last showing, and her recalling such facts made them feel special.

Max visited with people, introducing himself and talking about the paintings with such authority it was hard to believe he'd just learned about art. Elena smiled and turned, bumping into someone.

"I'm so sorry..."

Sokolov grabbed her arm. He jerked her closer and hissed, "The boss is here. If he hears anything about what happened at your apartment, I'll kill you and then your boyfriend." His hand tightened around her arm.

"Elena, darling. There you are." The woman she knew as Val walked up to her, smiling. She glanced at Sokolov and then down to his hand on her upper arm. "Is there a problem here? Should I call security?"

Sokolov blinked at the rare beauty in front of him. Elena could tell he was mesmerized by the woman's absolute radiance. Her white gown, white hair, and diamonds at her neck, dangling from her ears and clasped at her wrists, made her appear to be the winter snow maiden or Snegurochka. She looked like the pictures she'd seen in her children's books. All that was missing was a white fur hat and coat.

The woman frowned. "Please release my friend before I contact security."

Sokolov dropped his grip and bowed before throwing Elena a warning glance and walking away. Elena rubbed her arm, looking around to see if anyone else had noticed. "Thank you. I didn't see him come in, and your Russian is excellent."

"Thank you, and I saw him come in and make a direct line toward you. I'd hoped to intervene before he could get to you." Val took two glasses of champagne from a passing tray and handed her one.

A sudden hush from the crowd turned Elena. "Ah, my employer," she said as she accepted the champagne.

Val turned to look at the man. "The man of the hour."

"How much longer?" she asked.

"Not long. A white jacket, black slacks, and shoes. Black shirt and white tie," the woman described what her boss was wearing.

Elena frowned and looked at Val. "What?"

"Just admiring his taste in clothes. The black trifold kerchief in the jacket is impressive."

Elena frowned. "Somehow, I feel you're talking around things like Max does."

Val looked at her and smiled. "I think you'll do. You're sharp."

"Sharp?" Elena asked.

"Smart, on the ball," Val clarified. "I'll keep you in sight. Max needs you now." She moved away as Max walked up to her from behind. "I'd like you to introduce me now."

Elena set the entire flute of champagne on the tray of a server as they passed. "Sokolov warned me not to say anything about what happened in the apartment."

Max growled. A low, menacing sound only she could hear. "Val rescued me from him." She patted his arm as they walked the length of the venue.

They approached the group of people surrounding Abrasha. He was holding court. That was what she always called it. Now, she understood the fear in people's eyes. Now, she knew those people didn't accept the invitations because they wanted to be there. They accepted because not coming could lead to complications should Abrasha become upset. It was as if a film covering her perception had been peeled back, and she could see the truth instead of the story she'd believed.

When she could, she interjected, "Sir, may I introduce you to Max Stryker."

Abrasha turned to Max and smiled, extending his hand in the western custom. "A pleasure. I understand you're very influential in the art world."

All heads turned toward Max. He took Abrasha's hand, speaking with his American-tinged Russian accent. "A pleasure to meet you, sir. I also have the pleasure of telling you my boss will be here in about fifteen minutes and would like to meet with you about a certain investment."

"Perfect." Abrasha almost shouted the word. "This is something I'm very excited about. You'll inform me when the prince has arrived?"

Max's eyes darted from Abrasha to the crowd around him. "Ah ..."

"Do not worry. I have security, and no one here would *dare* repeat anything I say. Am I right?" He laughed and made a grandiose gesture as he turned to the crowd. A nervous ripple ran through the crowd, along with smattered words of agreement.

Max cocked his head to the left, and Elena felt her pulse quicken. That brilliant mind of Max's was processing. He lifted his chin and stated, "My employer is a private man, regardless of your assurances. Perhaps this was a mistake."

The humor on Abrasha's face fell away immediately. "Do not call off this meeting." Elena watched the crowd drift away. No, ran away. Everyone except Abrasha's bodyguards pretended to find the paintings suddenly interesting.

Max cleared his throat and squared his shoulders as if trying to give himself strength. "Do not broadcast my employer's title around as if it were a trophy for you to hoist in the air, sir."

Elena watched Max's eyes dart around nervously. So did Abrasha. The man smiled evilly. "If you insist."

Max nodded and then looked at her. "Would you like a refreshment, my dear?"

"I'd love one." They turned to leave, but Abrasha stopped her.

"Elena, a moment."

"Certainly." She stepped away from Max. "I'll be right there."

Max nodded and walked away.

"This man is not good enough for you." Abrasha sniffed as if he smelled something bad.

"Excuse me?" She blinked at his audacity.

"He's too weak. I can see it in his eyes. He has no steel in his body. You need someone who is strong." Abrasha extended his empty champagne glass, and one of his bodyguards filled the glass from a bottle they'd brought to the show. She'd always assumed it was because he had a favorite year or brand. Now, she realized it was his paranoia.

She glanced around them before answering, "I think I should be allowed to be with whom I choose."

"Of course, just know he is weak and a waste of your time. This one will not stand during bad times." Abrasha turned his back on her, dismissing her as he walked over to the only Pissarro he owned. Several couples flocked around him to compliment him on the art.

Elena turned around and walked over to where Max was waiting for her with a glass of sparkling water. "He told me you were weak and wouldn't stand during bad times." Taking the glass from Max, she turned her back on Abrasha. "How could I have not seen him for what he is?"

Max turned to look in the same direction, so his back was also to Abrasha. "The important thing is you see it now."

"I do." She nodded.

Max put his full glass on a small table meant for that purpose, then squeezed her hand. "It's time. Go with Val. Now."

Elena put the glass down and let go of his hand, heading straight for Val, who was watching her. She got to the door, and Val opened it. They both ducked out of the event room. "To the front parking lot. Do not stop."

Elena put her head down and walked as fast as humanly possible.

CHAPTER 22

Max watched Elena and Val leave the venue. Sokolov watched them but didn't follow. Max looked at his watch and spoke lowly. "Smith?"

"I'm here with Reaper." The reply came over the comms. "Malice?"

"Two seconds," Malice said. "Okay, all set. Driver's down. The key fob is in the driver's seat."

"Copy," Reaper said.

Max glanced at his watch again. Everything was going as planned. "I'm bringing him in." Max turned and made his way to Abrasha. He waited as the man pontificated about his acquisition of the Matisse, which was displayed perfectly. He reached down, clicked the crown of his watch, and waited.

Abrasha turned to him and smiled. "Is it time?"

"Indeed," Max said.

The people he spoke to moved away, and Abrasha's bodyguards moved closer—three now. He caught Sokolov answering his phone, and the man's head popped up. He looked over at Abrasha and headed in their direction. Max pointed to the exit. "This way, sir."

Sokolov rushed up to them. "Sir, a moment."

"I'm busy." Abrasha dismissed Sokolov.

"Sir, the vault. The fire alarm inside has activated," Sokolov hissed.

"Find Elena and get back there," Abrasha barked. "Take enough men to make sure my art is protected."

"Yes, sir." Sokolov barked out names, and five men charged toward the door, leaving two with Abrasha.

Max put his hand to his mouth. "Do you wish to delay this meeting, sir? Your art in Sochi …" He let his hand flutter about.

Abrasha gave him a dismissive look and scathed, "It is being cared for and insured. If the prince is here, I will meet him."

"If you insist," Max said timidly.

"I do," Abrasha spat at him.

"Please follow me." Max led him into the hallway

with the two guards at their heels. Max turned at the door. "Sir, if your men could wait here outside the door. There's only one way in and one way out, as I'm sure they are aware."

Abrasha looked at the men, then at Max. His left eye twitched, but he nodded his head. He turned to his guards. "Any sound out of the ordinary, and you're inside," he ordered.

Max opened the door and entered with Abrasha. A man in a white thawb stood in the corner facing the room.

The doors shut behind them, and Max's knife pushed against Abrasha's back. "One loud word, and you're dead."

The prince turned around. Abrasha paled. "Is this a joke?" he whispered as Smith disrobed.

"Indeed, it is not," Smith said, his voice almost a perfect replica of Abrasha's. What was perfect was the makeup that aged Smith to look exactly like his father.

"Who are you?" Abrasha's voice rose slightly, and Max shoved the knife a bit, causing the man to hiss.

"I'm your bastard." Smith walked up to Abrasha and looked at him as he took the robes off. He was wearing what Abrasha was wearing. Smith reached out and plucked the trifolded handkerchief from

Abrasha's pocket. "I never learned how to do a trifold." Smith put the folded fabric into his pocket. "Never had a father who gave a shit."

Abrasha's eyes narrowed. "What do you want?"

Smith snorted. "From you. Nothing." He put a bit of gravel in his voice, mimicking Abrasha's voice.

Reaper took the robes from Smith and handed them to Abrasha. "Put them on."

"What? Why?"

Max pushed the knife and felt it hit resistance. It had to have gone through the expensive jacket Abrasha was wearing. "If you want to live, put the fucking robes on."

Reaper lifted a handgun and pushed it against Abrasha's head. "I don't have the time or patience to tell you again."

Abrasha put on the robes, and Max reached into his pocket. He stuck the syringe into Abrasha and pushed the plunger.

Reaper holstered his weapon and bent over, taking Abrasha's weight over his shoulder. "Smith, you're up."

"Remember, Malice has your back."

"I'll be fine." Smith adjusted his sleeves under his jacket.

"Listen to them, Smith," Val growled.

"Are you safe?"

"We are," Val said. "Sokolov was looking for us but hasn't come into the forest. The blind is doing its job, and we're ready for pickup."

"Copy. Go." He nodded at Smith, who hunched over just a bit and walked out of the room. Instead of going to the venue, Smith turned toward the main lobby. The guards hurried after him. Max peeked into the hallway, waiting for Smith to take the guards.

"Let's go." Max led Reaper around the other corner and out the door toward the parking lot. He opened the back of the white van that was parked there early that afternoon and checked several times by staff security. Reaper flopped Abrasha into the back, then shut the door as Max dashed around to the driver's seat. Reaper sprinted across the parking lot toward the front of the hotel, where Smith would be waiting for Abrasha's car. Only the driver would be Reaper.

Max started the van and turned on the lights. He glanced at his watch and then put the vehicle into the drive as the first set of explosives blew. He floored the accelerator and zipped past the lodge's entryway.

Abrasha's guards had their weapons out as

Reaper pulled up right after Max. Max kept his eyes glued to the rearview as the guards pushed Smith into the car, and Reaper floored it out of the parking lot. Reaper turned left to pick up Val and Elena while Max continued straight for about a half mile before pulling into a wooded gravel road. He turned off the lights and the van before stepping out, taking off his tux, and shoving it into a bag before tossing the bag into the back of the van. From under the seat, he pulled out two packages. He took the thinnest and ripped it open.

Inside were overalls, socks, three pairs of gloves, and a t-shirt. He reached between the seats and pulled out a pair of boots, stomping into them before he gathered the second package and waited. It didn't take long before Malice ran through the opening and threw open the back of the van. His sniper's rifle was huge and heavy. Max watched as he pushed Abrasha out of the way and started disassembling the weapon before he put it into its case and then stripped out of his black clothing and put on the casual athletic attire waiting for him in the back of the van. He shut the back doors and walked to the driver's door. "Ready?"

"Yes." Maximus was more than ready. He went to the passenger side of the van and got in. Malice put the vehicle into reverse, and they were soon on the main road heading to the top of the mountain. They pulled up to the clearing Max had chosen, and Max tugged Abrasha out of the back of the van. He shut the doors and knocked twice on the van, and Malice drove away. Max watched the taillights until he couldn't see them anymore. Then he glanced down at the man at his feet. It was time for Abrasha Molchalin to pay for the evil he'd done. Max pulled the comm device out of his ear and placed it with the package holding his clean clothes.

ABRASHA WOKE UP WITH A JERK. Max leaned against a tree and watched as he tried to orient himself.

He noticed the position he was in and jerked at the ropes holding him. "Where are my clothes?" He looked around. "You! You pathetic little weasel. You'll get no ransom from my people!"

Max chuckled and walked closer. In English, he said, "This isn't a ransom situation, Abrasha. This is an execution."

The man stopped jerking at the ropes. "What?"

"You've been tried and convicted for your crimes

against humanity. The Council has decreed a death sentence for you. I am your executioner."

"I can make you wealthier than anyone else on the planet." Abrasha laughed. "You'd never have to worry about money again."

"I don't worry about money now." Max sat on the ground where Abrasha was tied belly down and strapped to two trees, keeping him in line.

"Who are you?" Abrasha's breathing sped up as he realized his situation.

"Today, I'm your executioner. Yesterday, I was an art dealer; before that, a computer specialist." Max sighed. "I made a study of the Vikings once. They were sadistic bastards, not only to their enemies but to other Vikings who'd lost their honor."

"I don't give a fuck about Vikings. Who are you?" Abrasha's spittle flew out and hung from his lips in a strand.

Max continued. "See, the Vikings had three particularly savage ways to eliminate those without honor. One is something they called hung meat. Basically, the Vikings cut a hole in your heels, run a rope through the holes, and then string you up. Upside down, all your blood will rush to your heart, and you will die. It is a slow, torturous way to go. But that isn't for you. The second method they favored was the death walk. I seriously considered this method. I would make a small incision in your gut, pull out a section of your intestine, and force you to walk around a tree until you are tied there with your guts. Savage and, again, a very slow way to die."

"Who are you!" Abrasha screamed.

Max ignored the man and continued, "But, for you, I think the Blood Eagle is the way to go."

Abrasha froze, and tears started to form in his eyes. "Who are you?" he whispered. "Don't do this. I can pay."

"I don't need money. Did you give any choice to the thousands you've had killed? To the children you've put into prostitution? To the people who've died because of your guns or drugs? What about your attempt to take over an entire country or explode dirty bombs in the earth's atmosphere to disrupt electronics and start World War III? You'd think you'd get the message that we wouldn't let you continue to be a threat to humanity."

"Tell me who you are!" Abrasha screamed.

Max looked at him. "I am a Shadow. *I am* the darkness you tried to emulate."

"A Shadow? They don't exist. They're a myth!" Abrasha laughed hysterically. "All right. The fun is over. Release me now, and I won't have you and your family killed."

Max reached over to a large crate and withdrew a knife and a short staff with a hook on the bottom. It would sever the man's ribs at the cartilage connection. "I am a Shadow. I am the Shadow who will send the message to your associates and the other monsters of the world that Guardian will never tolerate the abuse of those who cannot defend themselves."

"You can't be a Shadow," Abrasha cried out, jerking at the ropes holding him.

"I am, at least for this last mission. I am also the man who decided to let you die quickly. You see, shock will take you before I sever your rib cage from your spine or extract your lungs to let them flap outside of your chest cavity. If you have any prayers, now is the time." Max wouldn't deny anyone the chance to make right their afterlife.

"Fuck you!" Molchalin spat out.

Max stood up. "Abrasha Molchalin, you were supposed to be untouchable. You taunted the world with your despicable crimes. The world answered and found you guilty."

Abrasha's scream rang through the Caucasus Mountains.

CHAPTER 23

Elena and Val huddled in the small shelter of sticks and branches woven together. She heard Val tell someone they were ready for pickup as Sokolov was searching for them. She looked up and peeked through the branches back toward the lodge. Sokolov was running through the parking lot but finally called to the others, and they got into a dark SUV and sped out of the parking lot and around the corner before driving past them as they huddled not more than ten feet from the roadway.

"Well, that's the second step done. Let's hope the rest of the plan goes as well," Val said as she removed pins from her hair and groaned. "I hate updos." She ran her hands through her hair and looked over at her. "You did well. You're going to be fine."

Just then, an explosion shook the ground they were sitting on. A ball of fire went into the air.

"Oh my God!" Elena cried.

"It's happening. Watch," Val said, pointing to the parking lot down the hill. A white van flew out of the parking lot and drove away from them. Abrasha's Rolls was right after the white van but turned down the road that would bring it right past where they sat.

Val grabbed her hand. "Come on."

Elena followed her to the road, and the Rolls slammed on its brakes. Val opened the back door and pulled her into the interior. Elena landed in a heap on the floorboard as Val reached back over her and shut the door. Whoever was driving slammed on the accelerator, and they flew down the hill.

Elena's hair had tumbled out of its pins. She righted herself and pushed her hair out of her face. "No!" She backpedaled and pushed away from Abrasha.

Val held out her hand, and Abrasha helped her up. In English, Val said, "She's afraid of you, darling." She handed the man a large cloth, and he started wiping his face.

"I don't know how women wear this stuff," the man replied. "God, it itches when it doesn't feel slimy."

"Stop complaining, sweetheart. It isn't becoming. All ladies suffer through wearing makeup, and we don't bitch about it, do we?" she asked Elena.

Elena shook her head, watching as makeup started to cover the cloth. Val reached into the man's suit coat and pulled out a small pack of wipes. "Here, this will help."

The man took a wipe. He smiled at Elena. She couldn't believe what she was seeing. "You're … him …" She looked at Val. "But not." Elena pushed herself up into the seat. "What's going on?"

"This is my husband. He's a dead ringer for Abrasha, so we used that as a decoy. We had to age him a bit, but with the explosion, confusion, and rush, he passed as the old man." Val took a new wipe out of the pack and turned to her husband. "Let me. You're missing everything."

"Thank you." The man looked at Val like she'd placed the moon and stars in the sky.

Val kissed him and continued to clean his face.

Elena closed her eyes and shivered. The entire scene was surreal. She asked, "Did you get Abrasha?"

"Of course," Val said.

Elena stared out the window into the dark as they wound through the mountains. "Where are we going?"

"A safe house not too far from here. We'll wait for Max there," Val said. "Then we'll all go our separate ways."

"America," Elena said and closed her eyes. She was going to go with Max to America. She was going to work with the paintings—a new life, away from a monster who'd used his money to buy the stolen works.

She glanced at the couple when they slowed and then turned down a gravel road. Val's head rested on the man's shoulder. He was staring at her. "I'm sorry I scared you."

"You did shock me a bit," she said as the car hit a pothole and jolted them.

"Imagine how shocked we were when we found out he looked like that bastard," Val said without opening her eyes.

"I couldn't imagine. I saw some of the things he was responsible for." She shivered and ran her hands up and down her arms. "Are you related to him?"

The man shrugged. "Only by DNA."

Val opened her eyes and laughed. "His mom had an affair with Abrasha. His parents were troglodytes of the highest order. But he's smart. He survived, and I found him. Life has a way of working out. This is my husband, Smithson, or Smith for short, by the way."

Elena smiled at them. "It does, doesn't it? I never expected I'd meet Max."

Val smiled at her. "A pleasure. Are you going back to the States with him?"

"Yes, his people ... I guess they're your people, too ... offered me a job detailing the provenance of the stolen canvases and researching the history to try to determine the proper owner. It could take a long time to investigate each painting. There is a repository where art stolen during World War II is listed, but there aren't many pictures, so trying to match words to art is, to say the least, an inexact science."

"Guardian is an organization of integrity," Val's husband said. "Perhaps the last such bastion in the world."

Val glanced at her man. "They are," she agreed. Taking her hand in his, he smiled down at her.

"How long have you known each other?" They seemed so in love. "Did you meet because of Guardian?"

"Oh, that's a long story." Val chuckled. "I

kidnapped him one night, and we flew to Europe. One thing led to another, and we ended up here in Russia on a train. I think that's where we fell in love."

Smith shook his head. "I was in love with you the moment I met you."

Val smiled brilliantly at him. "You say the sweetest things!"

The car slowed to a crawl and then stopped. She looked outside but couldn't see much. "This is a safe house?"

Smith smiled. "This is where we park the vehicle. If they find the vehicle, they won't be able to find us or track where we've gone. It's best to be invisible. We'll wait for Max up the hill through the forest a bit."

Elena glanced down at her stiletto heels. "I wish I'd known that when I picked out these shoes."

Val chuckled. "I stashed our clothes yesterday. The guys will turn their backs, and we'll change to make the climb."

Elena let out a breath of air in relief. "Thank goodness. These are two-hour shoes."

Val's eyes widened. "You rate your shoes by the time you can wear them, too?"

"I do. I have all-day shoes, evening out shoes, and

then for these events, how long I can last without wanting to tear them off and throw them away."

Val clapped her hands. "You're going to fit right in."

"With who?" Elena asked as she followed Val out of the car.

"All of us. Max's people." She grabbed Elena's hand. "Come with me. Boys, find something interesting that way to look at." She pulled out a large black backpack and started handing Elena clothes. "I only met you once when you were hurt that night, but I guessed your size. I'm usually pretty good, but I erred on the side of larger for your hiking boots and brought two pairs of socks so if they were too big, you could manage until we got back to civilization."

Elena was grateful for the denim and long-sleeved shirt. She looked in amazement as Val pulled two sports bras out of the backpack. Val waved her off. "Girl, I've never been in a gown where I've worn an actual bra. I figured you'd need one, too."

She took the bra and laughed. "Thank you."

"No worries. Here, unzip me, and then I'll unzip you. Reaper and Smith won't look."

"Reaper?" she squeaked as she reached for Val's zipper. "Is that a real name?"

Val chuckled. "No, his name is Roman. We call

him all kinds of different names depending on his mood."

"I heard that!" the man she assumed was Reaper shouted from the other side of the car.

"Stop eavesdropping!" Val yelled back. "Turn around."

Elena did, and as soon as the zipper was down, she put on the sports bra. "Stand on your dress so your feet don't get dirty. There's nothing like having a stone in your boots. It sucks, especially going uphill."

"Are you speaking from experience?" Elena asked as she shimmied into a pair of jeans that were tight but not uncomfortably so. She had only one pair of denim she rarely wore because they were a status symbol in Russia—as were western trainers … um … tennis shoes. Why Americans called them tennis shoes instead of trainers she had no idea. She put on her shirt and pulled her hair out from the collar. She sat on her dress, put on her socks, and then the boots Val had brought. She stood up and tested the fit. "Perfect."

"Thank God. I was so worried I'd screwed it up. Smith would have had to carry you up, and I'd get jealous, but it would be my fault."

"Do you know you ramble?" the man on the other side of the car asked.

"Dude, are you still listening to us? I thought I told you to stop that." Val snorted and tightened the laces on her hiking boots.

"The crickets are boring. They don't tell any secrets," Reaper replied.

"Neither do I, asshat." Val stood up and stomped her jeans down. "You ready?"

Elena nodded. "Yes, what's an asshat?"

Val laughed. "Roman is an asshat. Grab your gown and shoes. We'll stuff them in here."

Elena winced at the way the material was shoved into the backpack. Her gown was expensive, but Val's had to be priceless.

"Okay, guys, let's go. I want a drink," Val called to the men.

The man she assumed was Reaper walked up to her and extended his hand. "I'm Roman, I'm not an asshat, contrary to Val's belief, and I told Max I'd make sure you got up the mountain safely."

"Hey, that's my job," Val said. "I told him I'd take care of her."

"You have, but it's all our responsibility to watch out for Max's lady," Val's husband said. "Ladies, shall we?"

"Thank you," Elena said.

Roman chuckled. "Elena, follow me. Grab my belt loops to help you get up the incline if needed. It's straight up in some places. Max said you were a tough lady, so we're going a route no one can track us."

Elena looked way up at the guy. His beard and the moonlight made him look a bit like a bear. She nodded. "I'm not too proud to accept help."

"Good girl," Roman said. "Let's go. Stay on my six."

"What?" Elena asked.

"Stay right behind him," Val translated.

"Is that an American saying?" Elena asked as they all started walking into the forest.

"Kind of. Military," Roman said from in front of her.

"Were you in the military?" she asked him.

"We've all been trained in military tactics," Val answered beside her. "We all have different backgrounds and circumstances that bring us to Guardian. They don't recruit based on your past. They recruit based on your ability and what you bring to the team."

"Like Max brings his ability to be anything." She

nodded, now understanding why he was with Guardian.

"His what?" Val said, slipping on a rock. "Shit."

"Give me your hand," Smith said to Val.

Elena grabbed her other hand and helped pull her up. "You know his ability to study anything and become it. He's looking forward to getting back to his computer systems."

"I bet he is," Roman said, reaching back for her. "Give me your hand."

She extended it, and he pulled her up about four feet to a small ledge. "Stay there until I get my next grip."

Elena looked down, and the moon's light showed her just how sharp the ledge was they had just scaled. "You weren't kidding when you said straight up."

Roman reached back for her. "It gets better."

She grabbed his hand with both of hers, using her legs to help lift her as he hauled her up. She wasn't sure how long they scaled the face of the mountain, but when Roman pulled her up onto a plateau, all four fell onto the ground and panted.

Val groaned. "I'm going to need to hit the gym a bit more."

Roman laughed. "I'm in the gym three hours a day, and that climb wiped my ass."

"Because you had to pull me up the mountain," Elena panted. "I'm sorry."

Roman lifted his head and looked over at her. "Something you'll learn, we'll do whatever it takes for one of ours."

"For as long as it takes," both Val and Smith said.

Elena stared up at the multitude of stars in the sky. "Do you think Max is okay?"

There was a pause before Val answered, "He's one of the best at what he does. Don't worry about him. He'll be here by tomorrow night."

"Tomorrow? Why not sooner?" Elena asked, sitting up.

"He has some loose ends to tie up," Roman said as he stood up. "A drink, food, and a soft bed are about a mile away. Shall we?"

Val's husband stood up and helped her up. Roman offered her a hand up, and she took it. They walked across a small field before she saw the farmhouse. Roman knocked on the door, and an elderly woman answered it. She smiled toothlessly. "Come, come in. Dinner is ready."

Reaper answered the woman in Russian. "Thank you, Grandmother. Your help is appreciated."

"My Ivan, he worked with Guardian before he died. I will always be here for you." The woman nodded and shuffled toward the kitchen. "It is only the dogs and me now. Guardian makes sure I am well cared for. I have food and money. They visit and check on me when they are in the country, as you do. Guardian cares. Russia does not."

Elena followed the elderly woman. "Grandmother, may I help you?"

The woman looked up at her. "You are Russian?"

"My father is; my mother is British."

"You leave Russia. Don't look back. Russia is dying. I have seen it with my eyes. Decay is a slow rot. Soon, the country will crumble." The woman nodded to an old fire-fed stove. "You can take the stew. Vodka is on the shelf." She shuffled to the cupboard to gather bowls.

Elena did as she was told and thought about the woman's words. She wasn't wrong. Sadness filled her. The country had such a history, but political corruption had caused a definite deterioration. She wished her father would leave the country, but he wouldn't. She listened to the laughter and fun of the people in the home. All spoke Russian perfectly. Guardian, it seemed, had resources and integrity. It helped an old woman who would have been alone and without resources. She counted her blessings and wondered where Max was at that moment.

CHAPTER 24

Max walked to the vehicle that had been hidden, opened the trunk, and took out three jugs of water and a bar of soap. Stripping, he washed the blood off his body. In the morning, the authorities would find Abrasha and his message. The field where the man had died was not far from the road. He'd be spotted as soon as the sun came up.

Of course, the death would not be mentioned on Russian news channels, but word would spread like wildfire. That was one thing the Russian government couldn't control. People talked, and they talked more when someone from the aristocracy was involved. Powerful, vicious people being humbled, or in that case, removed, was news, and word would spread faster than any government could manage.

He dried off, changed his clothes, and headed to Sochi. Max made no pretense about his movements. He parked in front of Elena's office, walked to the door, and looked up at the camera. He punched in the code to enter the office and walked in. Once inside, he said in English. "She's mine, she's safe, and your boss is dead. Come and get me, you bastard."

Max walked to the back loading bay, turned on the lights, and waited. He didn't have to wait long. The door from the office opened, and Sokolov walked in. Both men had guns trained on the other. "Abrasha is dead," Max said before he dropped his weapon's barrel.

Sokolov shut the door behind him. "Soon, you will be, too."

Max lifted away from the bench he was leaning on and placed his weapon on it. "Put your gun down and face me like a man, or would you prefer to beat up on a woman?"

Sokolov showed his teeth in a snarl. "She liked it." The man lifted his weapon's barrel to the ceiling and put it on a bench near him. Max moved to the middle of the bay at the same time as Sokolov.

Sokolov took a swing that Max dodged with ease.

The Russian moved again, testing his reach against Max. Max slapped the jab away. One thing he'd learned while training was that getting into a person's head or making them emotional was a definitive edge. Sokolov lunged, and Max danced out of his reach, slapping the man's face as he passed.

Sokolov growled and feigned with a right, followed by a left. Max ducked the punch and jabbed with a right. He felt the bastard's nose shatter under the force of his punch. Blood soaked the front of Sokolov's shirt. The Russian let out a shriek and dove for Max's knees.

Unable to move quickly enough, Max let the takedown happen and rolled, putting Sokolov on top of his shins, but with a poor grip. Max bent his knees, lifted his legs, and then kicked as hard as humanly possible, connecting in the junction of the neck and shoulder. He rolled away from Sokolov and sprung to his feet. Sokolov was quick getting up, too, but he'd hurt the fucker. His arm hung limply beside him, and blood continued to drip from his nose. In that instant, Max realized winning was no longer an option for Sokolov. How he died was.

Max smiled at the man. "Do you want to know what I did to Abrasha?"

Sokolov inched toward his weapon. Max countered the move and put himself between the weapon and the Russian. "Uh, uh, uh ... we were settling this like men. No guns."

Sokolov bolted for the bench and grabbed a screwdriver. He slashed at Max. The reach was just enough to snag his shirt and rip it. Max spun with the force of the slash and grabbed Sokolov's hand. Spinning, he brought the man's arm behind his back. Max stood behind the man and whispered, "I carved him up. Spread him open like a blood eagle. My people wanted to send a warning to everyone who preyed on innocent people."

Sokolov yelled and dropped to his knees. Max heard the shoulder pop out of its socket. He backed up as the man fell forward and slammed his shoulder into the floor's concrete surface. Sokolov lunged up and grabbed for his weapon.

Max pounced on the gun at the same time. His grip fell over Sokolov's on the weapon as they fell to the floor together. Grappling for control of the handgun, Max shoved his elbow into Sokolov's neck. He wrenched the gun at the same time as Sokolov squeezed the trigger. The gunshot didn't even register. Max pushed harder with his elbow. He felt the cartilage of Sokolov's neck give ... or maybe it was muscle.

He didn't care. Max twisted the gun violently and yanked it from Sokolov's hand. He stood up, panting and pointing the weapon at the bastard on the ground.

"Kill me!" Sokolov baited Max. "Shoot me and be done with it."

Max shook his head and walked over to the bench. He picked up a box cutter. "No. Shooting you would end your miserable life too early."

Sokolov spat blood at him and tried to get up. "My men will kill you as soon as you leave. You're a dead man."

Max laughed. "Your men are already dead." Or they would be shortly. Malice had been watching the office since he'd arrived the night before, and it was his job to eliminate anyone who might disturb Max's … fun.

"You won't get away with this." Sokolov lunged to his feet and swayed.

Max pointed to the post in the middle of the receiving bay. "Does that remind you of a tree?"

Sokolov looked at the post and then back at him. "What?"

"There is this method of killing the Vikings used for those who had no honor. You know, like men who beat defenseless women. Men who traffic children, who protect the scum of the earth, and kill indiscriminately. Men like you."

"Fuck you." Sokolov spat at him again.

Max wiped the blood-tinged spit from his face and lunged forward so quickly that Sokolov didn't realize what was happening. He made a deep cut in the man's abdomen with the box cutter. "It's time to take a walk."

* * *

AN HOUR LATER, Max walked out of the office to see Malice leaning against the white van. "Took you long enough."

Max entered the van, and Malice slid into the driver's seat. "He was stubborn in death." Max cocked his head to the left. "And now I know why the Vikings used those methods."

"Ah ... dare I ask?" Malice said as he pulled away from the curb.

Max shrugged. "Probably not."

"Copy. You sure there was no camera action last night?" Malice asked. "There are three very dead men scattered around this area, and I don't like pictures."

Max glanced over at him. "I disabled all cameras

in the area before the party last night. The only one working was above the door to Elena's office, and I will eliminate that footage."

"Dude, just how good are you with those electronics?" Mal asked as they started their journey out of Sochi.

"I'm the best." It was a simple statement that held the truth. No one had ever matched his ability with any system, and no one would. He reached into his pocket and pulled out his cell phone, dialing Archangel.

"Go."

"It's done."

Archangel's relieved sigh came over the line. "Status of operatives?"

"Malice and I are en route to our stand-down position. Once we're under the cover of darkness, we'll move to the safe house."

"Affirmative. Check in when you make contact, and I'll send the aircraft to retrieve you."

"Elena will be with me. She accepts your offer of employment."

"Good. Bring her home."

"Affirmative."

"Max?"

"Sir?"

"Did you send a message?" Archangel asked.

"A very ancient one. But one that is clearly visible."

"And this is your last mission?"

"Affirmative, sir. My last mission."

"Thank you for your service in this capacity, but thank God you're done with that portion of your life experience."

Max laughed. That was what he'd called going through the assassin's training when he'd told his father and Archangel he wanted to do it. Strange the man would remember that over the years. "Maximus is clear."

Malice looked over at him. "Your last mission?"

"As a Shadow, yes."

"But you're going to keep doing the computer shit?"

Max chuckled. "Yeah, I'm damn good at that shit."

"Better than Con ... hey, have you ever wanted to mess with someone?"

Max looked at him. "What do you mean?"

"Did you know Con put a kid's song on Fury's phone? Made it play louder and louder. It didn't start their feud, but, dude, it escalated it."

"I was not aware, no." Max chuckled. "Sounds like something Con would do."

"Right? I was thinking maybe payback would be sweet. Could you do something like that to Con's phone?"

Max snorted. "In a heartbeat."

Malice hooted with laughter. "But you got to wait until he's on a mission with us so we can witness it."

"Does he still go out into the field?" Max hadn't seen Con in the field lately.

"Don't know. I can let you know if it happens." Malice laughed. "Oh, man, that would be something to see."

Malice chatted about this and that. Max tuned him out and walked through the issue of supercooling that needed to be solved for his latest system. Although he answered appropriately when Malice asked him a question, he wasn't really present. That was until they hit the hill overlooking the field where Abrasha met his justice.

Malice slowed down and shook his head. "Fuck, man."

Max looked at the field. With a chemical spray, he'd written the Russian words "He is a warning." Each letter was at least ten feet tall, and at the top was Abrasha, sacrificed to the Viking gods for all to see. Vultures circled above the carcass. They could have him.

Malice kept the van going up the hill and looked over at Max. "What did you do to Sokolov?"

Max shrugged. "Took him for a walk."

"A walk?" Malice said and glanced in the rearview mirror. "Remind me never to go on a walk with you, okay?"

"Will do," Max said and closed his eyes. They'd ditch the van, move to a sheltered spot, and then get some sleep. That night, he'd be with Elena again. That physical and emotional connection welled inside him as if it were alive and needed her to continue to exist. He would feed and care for that connection until the day he died. He had no empathy for the men he'd killed. They were unimportant. Elena, however, was a critical piece of his world. Right then, she was the only thing that mattered. Well, Elena and solving the supercooling issue that he'd started working on when he tuned out Malice.

CHAPTER 25

*E*lena sat outside the small farmhouse. The others had told her Max would be there at sunset. The sun had set about an hour ago, and he still hadn't arrived. Val came out and sat down on the bench with her. "They'll be here."

Elena made a noncommittal noise and searched the darkness for Max and the other man.

Val leaned back. "Have you ever been to the States before?"

"No. I always hoped to move to London and take a position in a museum." She leaned back with Val and tried to relax, but it was almost impossible.

"New York has galleries and museums. I'm not sure where Max is home-based, but that would be a great job market for you after you find the owners of the paintings."

"He lives in New York," Elena told her. "How do you not know that?"

"Max is a specialist. We don't know much about him on purpose. If Guardian wanted us to know, we would. He trained with us, but he was separate. There were two in our group who were there but were held separately. It's weird but accurate." Val chuckled. "We're all weird in one way or another. Max just seemed to tune everything out. A couple of us thought he was on the spectrum."

Elena shook her head. "No. He was bored."

"Bored?" Val laughed. "Those were some of the most intense classes I've ever been through."

Elena shrugged. "He works on problems in his mind when he's bored." Or didn't have a connection with the people he was with, which was interesting. Max worked with those people, but he wasn't connected to them.

"There they are," Val said, standing up.

Elena was on her feet and running across the field. She launched at him, and Max caught her. "You're late," she cried as she held him tight.

"Late?" he asked as he held her. The other man

continued toward the farmhouse. "Was there a time set?"

She leaned back. "Sunset."

Max smiled at her. "Then I'm sorry. I would've been if I knew I needed to be here then."

"Is it over?" she asked, knowing he'd know what she meant.

"It is. Are you ready to start your new life?"

"I am. As long as I'm with you, I can do anything." She dropped her head again and held him tight. "I was so afraid something would happen, and you wouldn't be able to come to me."

"Hey, I'm here now."

She nodded, still holding him tight. "I was afraid for you. They were horrible men."

"They were," he agreed. "But we never need to worry about them again. Okay?"

She nodded. "When do we leave?"

"As soon as I call in and tell them we've arrived. They'll send an airplane for us."

"An airplane? Where will it land?"

"You didn't do much exploring today, did you?"

She shook her head. Her eyes had been glued to the horizon all day. "No. I just waited for you."

"Up behind the farmhouse is a flat field Guardian has used several times as an extraction point. Grandmother is crafty and will let her goats out in the field after we take off. The goats will obliterate any tracks left by the aircraft. Guardian provides for her and checks on her as much as they can. She won't leave, or we'd take her with us."

He took her hand, and they started walking to the house. "When we reach the States, we'll tell your father you're safe, and you can call your mom to let her know where you are."

"With you?"

"Yes."

"Max?"

"Yes?"

"What is your last name?"

"Olsen. My name is Max Olsen."

She smiled at him. "Mrs. Max Olsen. It has a ring to it."

He grabbed her and crushed her against his chest. "Are you asking me to marry you, Elena?"

"No ... yes ... will you?"

"As soon as we reach the States." Max dropped to kiss her, and she wrapped her arms around her neck. She'd never felt so safe in her life.

"That is what we're flying to Athens in?" Smith asked as the little plane circled for a landing, well under radar detection.

Max nodded. "That's an Eclipse 550 with a range of two thousand eighty-four kilometers. Seats seven."

"Seven normal people," Smith grumped. "We're larger than normal people." He looked at Reaper, Malice, and then Max. "It won't make it."

Max chuckled. "It's only just over fifteen hundred kilometers to Athens. Considering an average headwind and the extra weight per male in the plane, we'll make it with just over one hundred kilometers of gas to spare."

Smith turned to stare at Max. "Why? Did I have to know that? Couldn't you have just said we'll be fine?"

Val laughed and patted her husband's back. "We'll be fine, dear."

Malice narrowed his eyes. "Did you count our luggage? I'm not leaving this rifle. Anya made it for me, and I'll be damned if it stays."

"Cargo and fuel were calculated into the equation." Max shook his head. "Do you think I would get in if I didn't know it would make it?"

"Probably," both Reaper and Malice said.

Elena laughed and squeezed his hand. "I believe in your calculations."

"And you're the only one who matters."

"Hey, I matter," Val said.

"Not to him," Malice quipped.

"That's not nice," Val pouted.

"Here she comes." Max watched the small plane land and taxi up to them. They stowed Malice's weapon in the cargo hold, then entered the plane. Within three minutes, they were airborne again. Max looked down as Grandmother opened the gate for her goats. The pilot kept them low, under any radar detection capability, and they flew that way until they were out of Russian airspace. After that, they reached a comfortable cruising altitude and headed east. Elena slept against his shoulder as the day stretched on. As the lights of Athens appeared under them, he woke her. "We're almost there." He pointed at the lights below.

"The first step of our new life." She smiled excitedly. He studied her face. She was the most beautiful thing in the world, and he'd spend his life proving that fact to her.

"Our first step until our last on this earth. My heart is yours, forever." He kissed her softly, sealing his vow.

EPILOGUE

 EN YEARS LATER

MALICE WALKED through the crowded Atlanta airport. He'd missed his plane due to the weather and had three or four hours to kill. Sitting on those pieces of shit plastic chairs was akin to killing himself, so he walked and observed people. It was a habit he'd honed through the years. He frowned and stopped. Turning around, he met the eyes of a man he hadn't seen in years, although he'd heard him a couple of times when he was on particularly dicey missions.

"Max?" Malice walked over to him and extended his hand. "Damn, good to see you again."

Max smiled and extended his hand. "You aren't supposed to be here. Did you miss your plane?"

"Weather." Malice chuckled. "I won't ask how you knew that."

"Smart decision," Max agreed.

"Daddy, Daddy!" A small girl ran up to Max.

"Hey, princess. Where's Momma?"

"She's right there." The girl pointed to Elena. The woman's eyebrows popped up when she saw Malice. She walked up with a smaller boy in her arms. "Mal, it's good to see you again."

"Elena, you look wonderful." Mal kissed her cheek. "I take it married life agrees with both of you."

"It does indeed," Max said. "Honey, there are four seats available over there. Could you give us a minute to catch up?"

"Absolutely. Come on, sweetie. We'll go over and read a book."

"You'll come soon?" the little girl asked her dad as he set her down.

"Yes. Very soon," Max agreed, and Malice watched as Max tracked his family to their seats.

"How old are they?"

"Rachel is five going on seventeen, and Oliver is three. Whoever said it was the terrible twos has never dealt with a pissed-off three-year-old boy."

Malice laughed. "I have three boys myself. I agree. Three is the age of standing your ground even though you're dead wrong."

"Exactly." Max laughed. "I thought you were going to slow down. Heard you were opening two more shooting ranges with Anya."

Malice's eyes narrowed. "We just signed that paperwork last week."

Max shrugged, and Malice chuckled. "I've got five or ten more years in me. Too many villains and not enough good guys these days."

"Guardian keeps producing the good guys," Max said as he watched his family. "The baby class is exceptionally talented."

"The newest ones? Damn it, that makes my group the ancient ones now, doesn't it?"

Max chuckled. "You're the eldest of the classes, yes. Ancient? I'm not sure if that's an accurate assessment. But Jinx and the rest are in their prime now. The babies are just now entering training."

"Weird how recruitment is happening now, although it makes sense. And Lycos is long in the tooth, but he's damn good. Almost as good as Demos was."

Malice saw a smile flash across Max's face. "Demos was the best." Max crossed his arms and looked directly at him. "Guardian has evolved and changed. They've gone through growing pains and matured. Considering all the factors, we're going to be okay."

Malice chuckled. "Is that like you telling Smith it'll be okay when we got into that dinky airplane in Russia?"

Max chuckled. "Something like that. From the facts I have and knowing the personnel coming up and those overseeing our upcoming administration, Guardian has established a dynasty. It will last longer than any of us. Slowing down isn't a bad thing, Mal. Spend more time with your kids."

"I will, eventually. I still have that call, the need to be in the field."

"I can understand that, although thankfully, I've never had that desire again."

Malice nodded. "Well, I'll let you get back to your family. Are you headed to a vacation?"

"Florida and the Mouse." Max shook his head. "I get a lot of problems solved waiting in those lines."

Mal chuckled. "All I get is sunburned. Anyway, it was good to see you again."

Max cocked his head to the left. "I see you all the time, Mal. I watch over my own."

"If that came from anyone else, it would be creepy as hell."

"Guardian has a good staff at the helm." Max extended his hand. "It'll be interesting to see where they take the dynasty the company has become."

"It will be." He took Max's hand. "Whatever it takes, my friend. Keep watching, it's a comfort knowing you're there."

"I'll be watching as long as it takes," Max said. "And when it's time to step down, there is another who will do my job. Just like you."

Malice nodded and watched as Max went over to his family. He waved at Elena again and lost himself in the sea of people. A dynasty. Well, that was true, wasn't it? He wondered where the dynasty would lead Guardian in the years to come.

Want to read the first stories of the next generation of Guardians? Click below.

Legacy's Call
Legacy's Destiny
Throne of Secrets
Echoes and Oaths

ALSO BY KRIS MICHAELS

Kings of the Guardian Series
Jacob: Kings of the Guardian Book 1
Joseph: Kings of the Guardian Book 2
Adam: Kings of the Guardian Book 3
Jason: Kings of the Guardian Book 4
Jared: Kings of the Guardian Book 5
Jasmine: Kings of the Guardian Book 6
Chief: The Kings of Guardian Book 7
Jewell: Kings of the Guardian Book 8
Jade: Kings of the Guardian Book 9
Justin: Kings of the Guardian Book 10
Christmas with the Kings
Drake: Kings of the Guardian Book 11
Dixon: Kings of the Guardian Book 12
Passages: The Kings of Guardian Book 13
Promises: The Kings of Guardian Book 14
The Siege: Book One, The Kings of Guardian Book 15
The Siege: Book Two, The Kings of Guardian Book 16

A Backwater Blessing: A Kings of Guardian Crossover Novella

Montana Guardian: A Kings of Guardian Novella

Guardian Defenders Series

Gabriel

Maliki

John

Jeremiah

Frank

Creed

Sage

Bear

Billy

Elliot

Guardian Security Shadow World

Anubis (Guardian Shadow World Book 1)

Asp (Guardian Shadow World Book 2)

Lycos (Guardian Shadow World Book 3)

Thanatos (Guardian Shadow World Book 4)

Tempest (Guardian Shadow World Book 5)

Smoke (Guardian Shadow World Book 6)

Reaper (Guardian Shadow World Book 7)

Phoenix (Guardian Shadow World Book 8)

Valkyrie (Guardian Shadow World Book 9)

Flack (Guardian Shadow World Book 10)

Ice (Guardian Shadow World Book 11)

Malice (Guardian Shadow World Book 12)

Harbinger (Guardian Shadow World Book 13)

Centurion (Guardian Shadow World Book 14)

Maximus (Guardian Shadow World Book 15)

Hollister (A Guardian Crossover Series)

Andrew (Hollister-Book 1)

Searching for Home (A Hollister-Guardian Crossover Novel)

Zeke (Hollister-Book 2)

Declan (Hollister- Book 3)

A Home for Love (A Hollister Crossover Novel)

Ken (Hollister - Book 4)

Finally Home (A Hollister Crossover Novel)

Barry (Hollister - Book 5)

Hope City

Hope City - Brock

HOPE CITY - Brody- Book 3

Hope City - Ryker - Book 5

Hope City - Killian - Book 8

Hope City - Blayze - Book 10

The Long Road Home

Season One:

My Heart's Home

Season Two:

Searching for Home (A Hollister-Guardian Crossover Novel)

Season Three:

A Home for Love (A Hollister Crossover Novel)

Season Four:

Finally Home (A Hollister Crossover Novel)

STAND-ALONE NOVELS

A Heart's Desire - Stand Alone

Hot SEAL, Single Malt (SEALs in Paradise)

Hot SEAL, Savannah Nights (SEALs in Paradise)

Hot SEAL, Silent Knight (SEALs in Paradise)

Join my newsletter for fun updates and release information!

>>>Kris' Newsletter<<<

ABOUT THE AUTHOR

Kris Michaels' writing career is marked by 23 appearances on the USA Today Bestseller list and three on the Wall Street Journal Bestselling list for her full-length novels. As a writer, she is known for her compelling romantic stories set against military and law enforcement backdrops, as demonstrated in her series, The Kings of Guardian, Guardian Defenders, and Guardian Security Shadow World.

Originally from South Dakota, Kris's journey from a small-town high school to a twenty-two-year career in the military set the stage for her writing career, providing a wealth of experiences and backgrounds for her characters. Now living on the Gulf Coast, she writes full-time, focusing on creating stories that merge romantic elements with suspense and action. Kris explores the themes of love, duty, and bravery, which appeal to a wide audience.

Made in the USA
Middletown, DE
09 February 2025

71030464R00159